SOUTHERN FRIED STORIES

Tales of
Love, Lust, Booze and Chickens

a collection of short stories

by

J. R. Roseberry

Cover Design & Illustrations: Savannah Raines

Paperback ISBN: 978-1-959563-28-0
eBook ISBN: 978-1-959563-30-3

Published by:
Maudlin Pond Press
P.O. Box 53
Tybee Island, GA 31328
www.maudlinpond.com

Dedicated to all Book and Beach Lovers

Table of Contents

JAKE

The memory still awakens me some nights.

I sit up in bed sweating, but the salty liquid coating my body can never extinguish the unquenchable, searing flame burning in my belly.

Jake is always at the center of it.

He was a giant of a man with massive arms and a leonine mane of curly, reddish-brown hair atop his mammoth head.

My initial impression, when I spotted him lumbering through the bar late at night laughing, sometimes uproariously, seemingly to himself, was that he was a strange, hulking, clumsy drunk.

On closer scrutiny, however, he was neither clumsy nor drunk. He just moved differently, in a kind of tight, jerky motion, as though he was in a boxing ring, maybe even engaged in a bout as he moved… at least in his mind.

His was a taut, muscular grace, almost a dance if you watched him long enough.

Jake had an enormous, honestly-earned beer

belly protruding over his trousers and pressing hard against whatever ragged, once-white T-shirt he was wearing. But that bulbous belly was hard. It never bounced.

If pressed, you'd guess he was maybe in his late 40s, but age had no impact on his persona.

Everyone -- including the drunkest members of the mostly sodden beach crowd milling about Minnie's Bar -- edged out of Jake's way when he maneuvered through the room, laughing his odd, guttural laugh.

Even rare behemoths as big as Jake -- some sporting wider, weightlifter's shoulders over narrow, washboard abdomens -- stepped out of his way.

When I first saw their deferential movement, I was amused, then cautious. I reckoned they knew he was a handful. There was just something about him.

I met Jake on my initial visit to Minnie's place which sat in the middle of the dingy little business strip consisting mostly of bars, T-shirt shops, and rooming houses beside Tybee Island's main south-end beach, just down the road from Savannah, GA. He mounted the bar stool adjacent to mine and engulfed my left shoulder with his ham-sized hand, squeezing it with an uncomfortably firm grip.

Just before misplaced machismo prompted me to do something stupid, he grinned and muttered: "Name's Jake. Howzit goin'?"

Then, not waiting for an answer and wasting no more words, he turned toward Minnie who handed him a cold bottle of Budweiser before he sidled off through the haze of cigarette smoke to watch a game of eight ball on the nearby pool table.

Jake did a cursory cleanup around the place, wiping off tables and sweeping up after each day's 3 a.m. closing time, and it was he who encouraged stragglers to leave shortly after Minnie sounded the last call for drinks each night.

I never saw anyone fail to follow his suggestion to depart. Most were in such a hurry to comply that they spilled beer from the plastic cups cradled in their hands as they headed for the street.

Tybee was one of the last resorts on the East Coast which still allowed folks to sip alcoholic beverages any hour of the day or night on its public streets from what were affectionately called "go cups."

Grateful for his assistance, Minnie or one of her bartenders served Jake a steady supply of beer from about midnight on. Those were the wee hours when I haunted the bar strip, trying to capture the rhythm of the place and, occasionally,

conjure up a little non-committal, late hour com-
panionship.

I'd explain my nightly ritual away to friends
by telling them that I was gathering string for a
sometime story, while in truth I savored the taw-
dry, early morning bar action. A comfortable
feeling of being accepted by an alien group, being an inside outsider, warmed my innards like a
mellow swallow of aged bourbon on a cold night
up north.

Most of the sunburned, slightly saturated
tourists staggered off to bed by midnight while
the locals -- an assortment of redneck boozers,
many needing a hair of the dog when they awakened each day to control the shakes -- populated
the bars during these wee morning hours.

Their unpretentious lives appealed to me because, no matter how depressing or depraved,
they were real.

Walking towards the beach just after noon the
next day to purge the remnants of the barroom
booze and smoke from my brain, I spotted Jake
in the oceanside parking lot, leaning over the
open hood of a car, replacing its fan belt for an
overweight, balding tourist who stood nearby, his
frustrated, beet-red face bathed in perspiration.

Sauntering up to the shady side of the vehicle
I greeted him saying: "Howzit goin', Jake?"

Turning his big head sideways to look at me while his hands still worked with the belt, his wide grin clearly registering his delight that I remembered his name.

"Doin' good," he replied, then returned his attention to his work.

I watched for the few minutes it took him to complete the task. Then, while he wiped his hands with a filthy rag, I asked:

"Jesus, Jake, do you work all the time? You were at it after 3 this morning. How do you do it? I could hardly get myself to move today."

"Man's gotta work to eat," he responded, looking down at me from his six-foot, five-inch height while flashing a smile that lit up his face far more than the sunlight shining on it.

"I know what you mean," I said, before quickly padding off toward the surf to avoid an extended gap in what might have become an awkward attempt at conversation.

That night, and for several thereafter, I bought Jake a beer when I spotted him at the bar. Despite the fact that he was already drinking for free, the gesture seemed to please him enormously since it showed someone cared enough to buy him a drink with no quid pro quo, and it enabled him to bring in a little revenue for Minnie.

Beyond asking "Howzit goin'?" and saying "Thanks, Buddy", we never talked, usually just nodding toward one another or raising our glasses slightly in recognition. Still, there was an unmistakable, unspoken camaraderie.

Once, when Minnie served me ahead of a disheveled, half-drunk regular, the guy growled in my direction: "Who the shit's this punk?"

Before I could decide if or how to respond, Jake materialized beside the man, leaned close to his face and said in an even, stone-cold voice: "Dat's my buddy Jay. You gotta problem?"

The entire barroom became eerily silent in anticipation before the drunk muttered, very carefully, "No, no. Got no problem Jake. I jus' hadda bad thirst. Don't pay me no mind."

It was a comfort having Jake in your corner, but you could never completely relax with him around since he acted off-center strange sometimes, and you could never tell when he was one or two brews over the line since he always looked the same.

Once, when a bosomy blonde projecting prissy pretension strutted up to the bar, Jake turned to Minnie and mumbled: "I'd liketa see them babies inna wet T shirt!"

The woman squared her shoulders, thrusting her prominent breasts further forward while scowling at Jake as she replied scornfully: "Creep!"

Jake shook his beer bottle before leaning forward to spew the foaming liquid across the front of her blouse, thoroughly soaking it to reveal her clearly delineated nipples while the bar crowd roared its approval.

The horrified woman stumbled against several bar stools as she sped away, now moving in a streak rather than a strut.

The misbegotten night of my dreams occurred during the second week of my sojourn on Tybee.

I was sitting in my usual spot against the wall at the far end of the bar watching some college kids get a lesson in pool from a couple of filthy-fingered local fishermen on the coin-operated table beside the bar.

It was near closing time when one of the clean-cut but obviously inebriated collegians with "Vermont" stenciled across his T-shirt chuckled while leaning over to pick up one of the fishermen's pool balls which was blocking his partner's intended shot.

His action prompted his partner, along with four fellow students seated at a nearby table, to laugh uproariously.

Their laughter grew even louder when one of

the gnarled fishermen demanded to know: "What tha shit you think you're doin', kid?"

The laughter continued until the fisherman punched the offender in the face, sending him sprawling across the college boys' table, careening bouncing bottles helter-skelter before the youth hit the floor, his now misshapen nose spouting blood.

At the sound of the smashing glass, I reached unobtrusively for a pool cue, then hunkered down on my stool, back pressed against the wall, preparing to deal with whatever came my way.

The six now-suddenly-sober college boys grabbed beer bottles and started flailing away at the two gnarly fishermen who were swinging pool cues in whirling arcs at the heads of their attackers.

Two of the boys were instantly dropped while one of the fishermen was bleeding profusely, his ear partially severed, when Jake materialized.

Wading into the fray, he caught both pool cues in mid swing, yanking the sticks from the fisher-men's hands before banging their heads together and watching them sink to the floor.

That's when one of the college boys made the mistake of sneaking up behind Jake to break a beer bottle over his head. Shaking the broken glass from his hair, Jake wheeled around, picked the young man up above his chest and heaved him toward his friends, knocking the entire group down like so many bowling pins.

Two of the boys started to get up, but Jake just stepped on them while I winced at the sound of cracking ribs.

It was all over by the time the two policemen arrived, piercing the air with their whistles, waving their guns and screaming hysterically for everyone to get down.

Jake was standing in the middle of the mangled group of combatants, hardly even breathing heavily, when the older of the two cops, a grizzled goliath wearing sergeant's stripes, sneered, while waving a gun in one hand and a baton in the other, and shouted:

"Now I got you, Jake, you son of a bitch! You've finally fucked up, and I'm gonna put your sorry ass under the jail! Get the fuck into that squad car outside!"

Saying nothing, Jake started shuffling for the exit. He turned his head toward me, grinning and slowing down as he passed while patting the back of his trousers where there was the clear outline of a handgun.

When he could tell by my expression that I

saw it, he winked and moved on.

My mind whirled as I tried to process the situation, and I heard myself muttering, "Damn it!", convinced that Jake was going to shoot the cop before letting him put him in jail.

Jake's life would be wasted for nothing. So would the cop's. It was senseless! I had to do something to stop such stupidity!

The two policemen bracketed Jake, each holding onto one of his arms as they shoved him through the double-door exit.

Then, just as they reached the sidewalk, I rushed up to the younger cop and whispered in his ear: "He's got a gun. You've got to get it before someone gets hurt!"

To my amazement, the young officer screamed to his partner: "Watch out! He's got a gun!"

Jake turned to look at me in pained disbelief, his eyes asking sadly, "How could you betray me?" as clearly as if he had spoken the words, just before the air exploded with repeated blasts from the snarling sergeant's gun.

The first bullet smashed the window of his squad car; the second grazed Jake's head, and the third smashed into his right shoulder, spinning him around and hurling him against the side of the car as he fell while the sergeant stood over him shouting: "Sonufabitch! You fucking asshole!"

For me, the scene had suddenly turned surrealistic. Sounds and action moved in slow motion as the sergeant waved his gun, muttering garbled cuss words while the young cop's face turned white, his eyes bulging in disbelief, as he pressed his hands over his ears.

I imagined seeing the second bullet in flight as it passed through the skin of Jake's temple leaving a red ooze along its path, then becoming mesmerized by Jake's twirling movement after the third shot hit his shoulder.

It seemed choreographed, with a grimace etched over his face while his ham-sized hand inched toward the bloody mess of his right shoulder and he spun with a dancer's grace before thumping against the squad car and sliding slowly to the sidewalk, his handgun falling from his belt and bouncing on the pavement before skittering under the squad car.

Then the sergeant, his face distorted into a malicious mask, stood calmly over him as he fired another shot into Jake's unresisting body.

I was snapped from the dream-like scenario by the sure knowledge that this bastard was not done yet. He was going to empty his gun into the crumpled giant lying helpless at his feet!

Before he could squeeze off another round, I hurtled through the air, my scream of "Nooooo!" trailing off as I sailed toward the blue uniform.

My head buried into his gut causing him to drop his gun as his arms grabbed his stomach in pain before I swung my fist at his face with all my might.

I didn't know what I was doing but, propelled by adrenalin, was driven to stop this insanity or die trying.

I was wrestling the sergeant to the ground when the sound of an explosion caused me to roll over and look up.

There was Jake, who had somehow struggled to his feet, cold-cocked the younger cop, and was now leaning against the squad car for support, the young cop's gun in his left hand pointing directly at the sergeant.

The shot he had just fired hit the sidewalk an inch away from the older cop's head.

"No Jake! Don't do it!" I yelled before screaming for the sergeant to get the hell away while trying to help him up.

Jake calmly shot him in his left leg while I tugged.

He was about to fire again when I jumped up

to foolheartedly plant myself between the whimpering sergeant and Jake, looking him directly in the eyes while shouting, "Stop! For Christ's sake stop!"

Jake hesitated a moment, his eyes staring at me with the most sorrowful look I will ever know, before shoving me aside like an unwanted rag doll and struggling along the side of the car toward the sergeant.

The old cop had retrieved Jake's gun from under the car as he crawled around the vehicle and was now huddled on his knees, cringing in fear, staring at the toy pistol I had mistaken for a handgun when Jake approached, raising his weapon unsteadily.

I figure he could have gotten off another shot but was afraid he might hit me when I jumped between them, shouting again for Jake to stop.

There was really no need to, however.

The big man's legs collapsed, and the gun slipped from his fingers as he sank to the ground in excruciating pain, only his low grunt piercing the scene's silence.

I was kneeling beside him when his eyes turned glassy as he looked up at me and muttered: "Jay, buddy, howzit…"? his voice trailing off in a gurgle deep in his throat.

I lay down, pressing the side of my face into the growing puddle of blood covering his massive chest, clutching Jake in my arms as I wept uncontrollably.

I can't be sure, but I think I felt one last shudder as the final breath of life fought free from his heroic body.

That's what awakens me in the middle of the night now, sweating, sometimes weeping still.

JE T'ATTENDS,
MON AMOUR

Zoë Mon Amour

Sam stood in a quiet corner of the lobby, slouching slightly against one of the expansive lobby's giant marble pillars while slowly exhaling smoke from a cigarette held loosely between the fingers of his right hand.

Though his dark grey eyes were open, they had a glassy glaze, and he neither saw the dozens of people scurrying about him, nor heard the drone of their chatter.

Sam was a tall man inching close to 30 years of age. His curly black hair glowed with the same luster that now seemed to cover his eyes. Something about him, perhaps his large, lanky frame or that slight slouch and detached look set him apart from other men in the lobby.

Without knowing precisely why, one could tell at a glance that he was an American. Probably a Texan, most would guess, although Sam was born and bred in what he sometimes referred to as the "true South"… Savannah, Georgia.

An elderly gentleman interrupted Sam's solitary contemplation asking in a heavily-accented

French voice, "Could I have a light, Monsieur?"

"Certainly," replied Sam, slowly extending his arm to hand the stranger a silver cigarette lighter without bothering to look up.

The stranger lit his cigarette, then continued to stand there while he examined the lighter, silently reading its inscription: "I shall wait forever my Love, Yours Always, Zoë."

"She must have been quite exceptional," said the stranger.

"Pardon me," Sam replied, awakening from his mental stupor. "What did you say?"

"I said she must be an exceptional lady to wait forever," said the stranger, examining Sam's face with a sympathetic gaze as he returned the silver lighter.

"No, I'm sad to say," replied Sam. "She's no different from most. You see, she hasn't really waited, although I just discovered that here tonight."

"Tell me about it," said the older man, exhibiting genuine interest. "Perhaps things are not as bad as they seem."

"Actually, the story is a bit long and rather involved, but if you'd really care to hear it, I believe I might feel a little better just getting it off my chest," said Sam, his face creasing slightly with a melancholy smile.

"You see I was stationed here in France with the O.S.S. during the war working with your underground resistance fighters near Lyon, which was a major center for military rail traffic between Germany, France and Italy.

"We went out each night to destroy rails, hoping to cut off German supply lines. Lyon was also the site of one of the Germans' biggest troop concentrations, and we monitored all their movements, sending our reports to London each night by shortwave radio.

"We had numerous narrow escapes and lost a lot of good men during the few months my unit was stationed there. Our nerves became edgy, what with the Germans on all sides, and each day our fear of detection grew. My boys, many of them just teenagers, were about ready to break down under the constant pressure. I tried everything, but nothing seemed to lift their spirits.

"That's when Zoë arrived.

"At first, we thought she might be a German spy, and we refused to reveal our true identities, but after she gave us her credentials and offered vital support at the time we needed it most, we decided to take the chance, feeling we could hardly refuse and had little other choice.

"She proved to be a tremendous help immediately, serving as a guide since she knew the country well and was familiar with our situation having worked with the French Resistance since the Germans first invaded her homeland.

"Although she was indispensable as a guide, she was even more of a Godsend for the way she quickly soothed our spirits. She had the voice of an angel and would sing for hours on end providing a much-needed cloak of emotional comfort for each of us.

"Just as important, Zoë tended our wounded better than any combat medic we had ever seen. She was truly more valuable to the unit that any ten of us combined.

"We talked quietly through those long, lonely nights discussing our past lives as well as our hopes for the future if we were lucky enough to survive the war. Given that we were in jeopardy every moment, each of us knowing full well our odds of survival were relatively remote, we saw no reason for pretense or need for secrets.

"Zoë was so refreshingly open about her past and her hopes and feelings that she prompted a similar, although very unusual, openness from me as well.

"She told me about her unrealistic dream of becoming both a playwright and a stage actress after the war and that her ultimate ambition was to one day to appear in a musical production that she, herself, would write, featuring her as the lead singer. She said that in the best of all worlds her play would be staged in a major theater in Paris.

"We were attracted to one another from the start, but both of us fought against any emotional involvement since we were keenly aware of the futility and heartaches involved in wartime romances.

"Despite my best efforts, however, I fell hopelessly in love… and then came the Allied invasion sweeping across France like a blanket of hope for most but a somewhat bittersweet occurrence for me.

"I was ordered back the States immediately, my mission having been completed but still shrouded in government secrecy. I shared the information with Zoë as soon as I got the orders, vowing to desert so I could stay with her in France.

"But Zoë would have none of it. She said our love was perfect and must remain so, insisting that it could not now be based on deception or our having to look over our shoulders for the rest of our lives. She said we would simply take a brief break while I returned stateside to be discharged, settle my affairs at home and then rejoin her in France where we could start our new life free and clear.

"I'll never forget that last night we spent together. She had always been enchantingly lovely, but that night, with her golden hair flowing over her creamy white shoulders while tears of joy and sadness streamed from her pale blue eyes, hers was an angelic beauty beyond description.

"After kissing me tenderly goodbye the next morning, she extended her hand to me as my train pulled away, placing that silver lighter in mine.

"I can still hear her calling after me, 'Hurry back, my darling, please hurry. I'll wait for you Sam, my Love.'"

"That's the last I ever saw of her. It's been four years now. That's a long time to expect anyone to wait I suppose, but I spent virtually every moment of that time thinking about Zoë and concentrating on how I could get back to her.

"When I was finally able to return to France six months ago, I had no address for Zoë so I went back to Lyon hoping I could find her there. I spent weeks asking dozens of people there if they knew anything about her to no avail before I remembered what she said regarding her theatrical dreams.

"I finally located a theater company that told

me Zoë was now a fledgling new French theatrical light who was making waves as both a writer and actress, and I've spent the last several months apparently one town behind her as she moved from town to town and theater to theater throughout France.

"Each new theater was a bit bigger and a bit better, and now she is right here at the largest theater in Paris, just like she dreamed she would be. She's a star now, the talk of the town, and has no need for me. I doubt that she would even remember my name.

"I came to see her play tonight hoping to just get a glimpse of her and discovered how little she really cared for me. She's made a mockery of our romance through this play. Did you not notice? It's a war story and describes almost perfectly the events I have just related to you. I had to leave during the performance. I couldn't bear to see her make light of what had meant so much to me."

"Yes, I did notice the similarity, but I believe you are sadly mistaken, my young friend," replied the stranger. "I understand your depression but in your despair, you missed the ending."

"By the way, did you not see the title?"

"I saw it but I'm unable to read French," said Sam. "Her name was all I recognized."

"The free translation is 'Still waiting for Sam. Hurry back, my Love,'" said the stranger before slowly shuffling away.

Helen

She was something alright, no question about it.

She wasn't one of those so-called free-ranging, manicured-lawn-strolling, citified chickens that have become the pets du jour of the supercilious society set living in fashionable historic sections of Savannah.

No, Helen was the real deal.

She introduced herself one day by sauntering slowly into the yard of my cabin beside the Ogeechee River, on the south side of the city.

At first glance she seemed nondescript, somewhat smaller than a standard-sized chicken, and was covered with dull, matted-down black and red feathers.

What stood out about her were the eyes. Something suggesting curious intelligence lurked behind those shiny brown beads.

I was hooked when she first flashed them at me, abandoning the balky lawnmower I was fiddling with to mosey over to a bag of bird seed I had stashed near my picnic table.

Helen backed up when I took a step toward her while proffering a handful of seed. When I stopped, she did as well, but with each step forward she backed up again.

It was a Mexican standoff.

I finally conceded, placing the seed on the ground and backing away.

Helen had won the first round.

I later learned that victory was routine for this plucky pullet.

After finishing off the bird seed -- eyeing me between bites -- she strutted off, wagging her tail feathers, not indicating gratitude but proclaiming she deserved the meal, though the service left something to be desired.

I watched her, wondering where she came from, while she ambled around the perimeter of the property, crossed the dirt road behind the cabin, and cautiously inspected the edge of the swamp beyond.

There were only a handful of houses in my riverside community, and, like me, most owners came down only on weekends or holidays.

None kept chickens.

"God only knows," I mused, then forgot about

her and returned to my chores.

I went to bed exhausted that night but awakened, as usual, at the crack of dawn.

This morning, however, I was startled awake by the noise made by a large bird flapping its wings as it emerged from the big birch tree beside my second-floor bedroom window.

Staring out the window, I was amazed when I saw Helen. I had no idea she could fly, let alone that she might sleep in a tree!

Slipping on some shorts, I headed downstairs, figuring since she had almost been a bedmate, I ought to at least feed her.

She was standing right where I fed her the previous day, clucking cheerfully as I circled slowly around her to get the bird seed.

Since rain was threatening, I put a scoop under the gazebo sheltering my riverside picnic area.

Helen eyed me incredulously, waiting until I moved 20 feet away before approaching the food. Then, feigning only mild interest, she ambled up and snaffled it down with abandon after a tentative first peck.

This became the spot where I left her breakfast each morning I stayed at the cabin.

And every evening, just after sunset, I watched

her fly majestically up into the tree by my bedroom window.

Each day she let me linger a little closer as she ate, and each morning she began waiting outside my door, then followed several feet behind me while I fetched the seed sack.

I started reading in my living room at night, rather than in bed, telling myself it was better for my eyes to sit up but knowing deep down that I didn't want my bedside light to disturb Helen's sleep by shining on the tree where she perched.

When I was away for days at a time, I figured she would wander off to find a more reliable benefactor, but each time I returned, she emerged from somewhere to stand by the car, clucking repeatedly either to greet me or chastise me for my absence.

I learned a lot about Helen that first summer.

Twice each day she cleaned herself by scratching out bowl-sized holes in the ground and wallowing in them, then fluffing up her feathers and flapping her wings to shake off the sand.

Helen's version of a daily shower seemed to work very well. Her feathers developed a healthy sheen, her comb turned bright red, and she was never bothered by mites.

She was a first-class forager, scratching up

juicy worms when the soil was damp with dew in the morning or any time after it rained, and ferreting out small bugs and caterpillars from bushes when it was dry.

If thirsty, she ambled down the rocks by the river, dipping her beak in the water when I forgot to fill her bowl.

And she had no problem protecting herself from either wild or domestic creatures in the neighborhood.

Helen was always on the lookout for a pair of huge hawks nesting in a tall, swampside cypress tree across the road.

Whenever they left their nest, she would strut toward the cabin and squeeze through a hole she had found in the wood lattice enclosing the crawl space underneath.

She never rushed, but always managed to reach safety before the hawks were ready to dive.

Even the free-roaming neighborhood dogs proved no problem for Helen.

When they charged toward her at full bark, she simply took to the sky, soaring to a nearby tree from where she emitted clucks that sounded almost like a chuckle while the dogs circled below, yelping themselves hoarse.

Ultimately, the dogs gave up and settled for a permanent truce.

Another victory for Helen!

One thing she wouldn't do is eat regular chicken chow.

She insisted on bird seed… the more expensive the better.

I found that out the hard way when I bought a 50-pound sack of special chicken chow recommended by the manager of a farm food store I had searched for days to find.

After Helen repeatedly rebuffed the proffered feed, scratching up her own bugs and worms for a meal when the chow was all I offered, I tossed it into the river, hoping fish were less finicky about their menu than my fine feathered friend.

By summer's end she was a flying, hopping, scratching bundle of energy looking altogether radiant though, truth be told, my growing admiration may have contributed to Helen's rapid transformation from a bedraggled hen into a beautiful bird.

As winter approached that first year I grew concerned, having heard that chickens couldn't survive outside in frigid weather and had to be housed in a heated coop.

I laboriously built what I thought might suffice for one, using treated wood and wire, filled the floor with pine straw and placed it on cinder blocks under the house, taking care to turn the entrance away from the prevailing wind.

If it got really cold, I figured I could run an extension cord to my makeshift coop and hook up a light bulb to provide warmth.

While Helen watched, I placed a heaping handful of seed in front of and just inside the coop hoping to lure her into her new home.

She ate the food but disdained the shelter, preferring to sleep in her tree. She slept there each night throughout the winter, regardless of the temperature.

And she survived quite handily, scratching right through frost covered foliage for hidden morsels when she needed a snack.

The next summer my cabin visits became more frequent for some reason, and Helen seemed to thrive.

But one weekend when I returned, she wasn't there to meet me.

I searched under the house and beside the river and swamp, then spent the entire afternoon walking up and down the road calling her name but could find no sign of her.

My neighbors must have thought I was crazy out there patrolling the neighborhood calling a chicken by name.

Crestfallen and trying to convince myself her apparent demise was simply nature's way and, after all, she was just a chicken, I shuffled back to my cabin.

There, lo and behold, stood Helen on the precise spot we agreed she would take her meals.

Her head was drooping, her feathers dull and matted. She was the most forlorn, bedraggled looking hen imaginable.

But despite her appearance, I was elated to see her. My eyes began to water for some reason as I fairly skipped over to fetch her food.

Helen was so tired she didn't even move as I placed a handful of seed at her feet where she gobbled it up before wobbling off up the road.

Curious about where she was heading and how she had become so disheveled, I followed about 50 feet behind. Each time she stopped to stare at me, I stopped, in a scenario reminiscent of our initial meeting. She wandered, apparently aimlessly, several hundred feet up the road, then began scratching around the base of a bush while I waited, and waited, and waited.

I finally gave up and returned to the cabin to

have a drink and relax on my porch overlooking the river.

A half hour later I spotted Helen. She was moving stealthily along the river bank in a direction opposite to the one where she had led me.

I remained motionless until she passed, then crept silently to the edge of the porch to watch her continue her stroll beside the river.

When she reached my neighbor's yard a hundred feet away, she stopped, peered cautiously in every direction, then ducked under the carport where my neighbor kept his boat.

As far as I could tell, she didn't emerge for the rest of the weekend.

When I returned a week later, she appeared once more at her feeding area, and we engaged in the same scenario, with her leading me far up the road, then stopping to scratch until I left.

This time, I returned to the cabin immediately, pretending to go inside; then sneaking stealthily over to my neighbor's carport.

There, under the steering console of his little boat, I found a nest with ten small eggs.

Helen had been hunkering down there, going without food or water for days at a time, in an utterly futile effort to hatch her infertile eggs.

Concerned for her health should she continue to deprive herself with this pointless vigil, I gathered up the weeks-old eggs and tossed them into the river.

She spotted me just as I hurled the last one in, then scrambled angrily to the empty nest where she screamed in anguish for an hour.

Helen hid from me the next two days, seething with anger toward the man she considered her children's executioner, but finally relented, grudgingly accepting the seeds I offered as long as I kept my distance.

I pondered the situation for several days before hatching an idea. I would buy some fertilized eggs from the farm store and let Helen sit on them. Hopefully, this would satisfy her maternal instinct without ruining her health.

After placing the eggs in a nest of soft rags and leaves in the unused coop, I sprinkled bird seed inside the entrance while Helen watched, assuming the prospective mother would squat as nature intended when she saw the eggs.

When I stepped away, she stared at the eggs, sniffed them disdainfully, ate the bird seed and strutted away.

Helen slept in the tree again that night, and as far as I know, she never looked at those eggs again.

A week later she watched as I tossed them in the river. It didn't seem to bother her at all.

Shortly thereafter, we were at it again.

Helen would find a hiding place, build a nest, lay eggs and sit on them, depriving herself of food and water in a futile effort to hatch a family until I found her nest and destroyed the infertile eggs.

I was at my wit's end, figuring our hunt-and-destroy egg expeditions might go on forever when, wonder of wonders, salvation suddenly arrived in the form of a rooster strutting into the yard from parts unknown.

While small, this guy was unbelievably handsome, sporting a bright orange wattle, and full, upswept tail feathers of orange, black, red and gold.

He damned well knew it too, strutting around the yard, cocky as you please, while displaying his plumage from every possible angle.

I figured Helen would be smitten instantly, but I never could read that lady's mind.

She clucked a harsh rebuke when he rushed up to her, then batted him away with her wings.

He was crestfallen when she rejected his advances and took to padding around after her with a hangdog look for the next several days.

This was a rooster who was all looks and no brain. He reminded me of some of those barroom cowboys parading around Tybee Island watering holes every Saturday night.

Clem, the name I generously dubbed him after first considering Doofus, turned out to be useless.

Helen had to show him where to find bugs and worms, often digging them up for him.

She even had to teach him to fly.

Each day at sunset she flew majestically up to her perch from where she clucked frantic directions to Clem who stood squawking forlornly at the base of the tree.

Then Helen would fly to the ground, goad him with stern clucks, then hop/fly to a low branch.

After a week of this, Clem finally mustered the courage to leap to the lowest limb beside her. Then Helen hopped to the next higher limb, laboriously luring Clem up again.

Clem got a little higher each evening with his hop/fly effort before finally realizing he could fly all the way up to the final perch from the ground.

After that, he strutted around at sunset, pretending to direct Helen to the perch before flying up himself and fussily wriggling down in the comfortable crook of a tree branch.

It was Helen who helped him evade the hawks, which Clem never seemed to notice until she bumped him in the butt, pushing him towards the gap in the lattice.

Clem's gravest mistake… one which Helen could not correct… was his constant heralding of the moon or stars or whatever mirage he conjured up with ear-splitting "cock-a-doodle-doos" in the middle of the night.

His raucous squawking often continued intermittently until dawn.

I yelled at him, threw shoes at him and even took pops at him with a little BB gun I used to scare squirrels away, but nothing shut him up.

Eventually, Clem and Helen managed to mate.

I'm betting she had to give him instructions.

After their soiree, it took me a week to find her nest. It was in the same boat, which my neighbor had covered with a canvas tarp after discovering the telltale feathers Helen had previously left inside.

I walked by that boat a half dozen times before accidentally catching a glimpse of her head popping out from under a loose spot in the canvas.

Spotting me, she quickly ducked back inside

the boat.

Carefully easing the cover off, I saw her in a cranny near the bow, feathers fluffed up and wings spread wide to hide the eight eggs on which she was sitting.

That's when I heard a faint "peep" coming from beneath one of her wings.

Her chicks were arriving!

Dashing back to the cabin, I grabbed a beach towel and plastic bucket, then jogged back to the boat.

Turning back the canvas cover, I gently spread the towel over Helen and lifted her from the nest.

Then I picked up the chicks… three had now hatched… and the remaining five eggs, tenderly placing these in the bucket before heading home, speaking softly to Helen all the way in an effort to comfort her.

She seemed to understand since she made no noise and did not struggle on the long walk.

Once there, I placed the eggs and chicks in the coop under the house and released Helen. She squawked only once before hopping in and squatting tenderly down on the nest.

I spent the rest of the day cleaning egg shells, poop and feathers from my neighbor's boat, hoping he would never know it had been used as Helen's nursery.

Three days later, while I was sitting outside, basking in the early summer sun, Helen stepped gingerly into the yard with eight chicks stumbling along behind her.

My grin grew so wide it hurt my face. I felt like a proud father!

Over the next several weeks Clem bumbled about trying to entice Helen to once more do what she had apparently taught him only to be repeatedly rejected, often quite forcefully.

Helen turned out to be the perfect mother.

She stayed close to her chicks, watching their every move while showing them the best spots to scratch for bugs and worms; leading them to the river where she taught them how to dip their beaks in for a drink, and showing them how to take sand baths.

When they were a month old, she led them to the bird seed I put out, but always held them back until I moved away from the site.

I was a bit offended because she didn't seem to trust me around the kids but finally decided it was probably a valuable lesson in case they ever came in contact with an unfriendly human.

Clem, without the constant protection of Helen who was now too busy fending for her chicks to look after him, grew more and more vulnerable.

He seemed incapable of scratching up his own meals, depending on me for both food and water. And without Helen's protection, he was pretty much defenseless.

That dependence led inexorably to his demise.

One day when Helen was teaching her brood to scratch beneath a bush beside the house, Clem wandered down the road, oblivious, as usual, to everything around him.

That's when the hawk swooped down and carried the frantically squealing rooster away.

While Helen may not have been happy about his departure, she didn't seem particularly perturbed, using the traumatic situation as a teaching experience for her kids.

From that moment on, whenever she spotted the hawks, Helen would utter an almost inaudible cluck and all her chicks instantly squatted, becoming almost invisible in the tall grass while their mother sauntered further and further away from them to duck under the house or a nearby shed while the hawks watched her in vain.

The brood remained still as statues until their

mother returned to give them the all-clear sign, after which they resumed their foraging as though nothing had happened.

As for me, I missed Clem's beauty and the occasional humor he evoked with his bumbling ways, but I was not at all saddened by the absence of those midnight cock-a-doodle-doos.

Under Helen's love and careful tutelage, the chicks thrived.

They made a game out of hiding and staying put at their mother's direction, even when nothing seemed to be around, and they were soon digging up their own grubs.

The chicks even made it up to the roost on their own each evening, hop/flying from limb to limb like Clem used to do, and flapping awkwardly all the way down each morning.

Now I started worrying about having eight adolescent chicks and a mother hen roaming around the neighborhood, particularly when nearby property owners and their children and friends came down on holiday weekends.

I decided I had to round up the brood and take them to a farm where they might live happily without bothering, or being bothered by, anyone.

But catching them turned out to be a problem.

First I tried chasing individual chickens down but the half-grown, all-wild birds were too quick for me as they dashed, half flying, to safety in the nearby swamp.

All I got for my trouble were cuts and bruises on my legs after slipping and falling over rocks and tree roots during the chase.

Then I recalled my childhood when I lived with my family on a small farm and learned to trap birds and rabbits.

I figured these same techniques should work with the chickens.

Rigging a wire cage with a spring-loaded door held open by a string tied to a post beside a chair 30 feet away, I sprinkled bird seed just inside the cage, then sat in the chair, ready to yank the string to let the door snap shut as soon as the brood entered.

Helen and the chicks came to the cage alright, but they just leaned over the entrance to eat the seed they could reach, then wandered away to forage for worms.

At first I thought this was an aberration, but after trying the same ploy unsuccessfully four days in a row, I was convinced that Helen had told her chicks not to enter that cage.

She had outsmarted me again.

My next effort was to try trapping the birds under the cast net I used to catch shrimp the previous summer.

Armed with the carefully folded net at the ready I stood nonchalantly near their regular mound of birdseed, waiting patiently until the entire family was busy pecking away at their meal before hurling the net high over the unsuspecting flock.

The net hit the ground with a loud thud, and I raised my arms in triumph before realizing that all except two chicks had escaped with Helen, who had wriggled free, before holding up the edge of the net with her body while all except the last two scrambled out.

I rushed back to the cabin to get a towel to throw over the last two chicks, but by the time I got back, Helen had somehow freed them as well.

She greeted my approach with strident squawks, letting me know what a lowlife I was before herding her progeny off towards the swamp.

That's when I gave up further attempts to outsmart Helen and her chicks and was reconciled to letting their tenuous living arrangement play out on her terms.

Now defiant, Helen and her family started sleeping in another tree beside the swamp on the far side of the road.

While their move may have assuaged Helen's anger, it created a perilous situation for her kids and ended my worries about their running wild through the neighborhood.

The adolescent birds disappeared one at a time over a period of several weeks, kidnapped in the dark of night, I supposed, by a possum, coon, or snake.

Ultimately, only Helen, her daughter, Henrietta, and Clem Jr. remained.

Clem Jr. grew up to be even more handsome than his dad.

Happily, he inherited his mother's brains, becoming a great forager and fantastic flyer.

He led both Helen and his sister to a higher and safer nighttime roost in a huge old moss-draped cypress tree beside the river.

Unfortunately, he inherited his feather-brained father's least desirable habit… those uncontrollable, untimely cock-a-doodle-doos.

While he was smart enough to quickly scurry out of range whenever he heard me cock my little BB gun, it was this infuriating penchant that eventually did him in.

He was on a neighbor's porch at 3 a.m. when

he decided to loudly greet a glorious full moon. A moon so bright, I suppose, that he found it irresistible.

It was also bright enough to clearly spotlight this handsome rooster on the porch rail, and it was during the brief pause between his shrill cock-a-doodle greetings that I heard the crack of the rifle followed by the sound of silence.

I knew instantly what had happened, but I couldn't really blame the neighbor, having considered taking the same action several times myself, restrained only by the fact that I couldn't muster the courage to face what I was sure would be a monstrous guilt complex if I actually did the deed.

Henrietta passed away that winter, unable to handle the freezing temperatures which had never bothered her mom.

Helen, however, continued to thrive.

I took comfort in the fact that she settled back each evening onto her old perch in the tree beside my bedroom window, and I got pretty good at finding her constantly-changing nests and clearing out the infertile eggs.

Thankfully, her nesting lessened, eventually occurring only a couple of times each summer.

She lost a step or two and began to suffer from

diminished vision near the end of her eighth year with me. She also lost some of her deft touch for foraging, causing her to rely on me more and more for food and water.

This weighty responsibility led me to stay at the cabin most of the time now.

Helen started settling down on lower limbs of the tree that year, apparently unable to make it any higher.

I empathized with her more than I wanted to admit.

It was getting harder and harder for me to climb the cabin stairs, and, often after feeding my feathered friend, I found myself sitting in the rocker on the porch overlooking the river, reflecting on the fact that we were quietly growing old together.

When Helen failed to show up for her meal one morning, I figured she had laid another of her infertile batches of eggs and shuffled out in search of her latest nest.

I never did find it.

But I did find Helen.

She was in an open area beside the swamp, just a little pile of bones and reddish-brown feathers surrounded by a bunch of bigger, grey and white feathers, like those of the hawks who had hunted her for so many years.

They had finally caught up with Helen, but they had to wait until she was an old, old lady to do it.

Even then she apparently gave them the fight of their lives.

They didn't even try to feast on her remains.

Maybe they were too injured to do so -- or perhaps they left her in peace as a tribute to her heroic efforts over the years, right down to her very last breath.

Maybe Helen even let the hawks win because she just didn't want to face another winter alone… didn't think it would be dignified at her age to hunker down, shivering in the cold.

That would be like that grand old lady.

I miss my feathered friend. I still can't bring myself to read in bed at night with the light shining out on her old roost.

Helen was something else alright. She was the real deal.

Confessions

It's been a long time since I've cried, so long, I suppose that I can't any more.

God knows I felt like it when she told me.

I had the difficulty breathing, the queasy feeling, the blurry eyes… but no tears. They just wouldn't come.

And even those other reflexes were delayed, buffered as they had been for years either through subconscious self-preservation or insufficient emotional trauma to trip the intricate mechanism releasing them.

My initial reaction was to question, almost academically, the facts surrounding her disclosure.

Where did it happen? When? Who was involved? Who knew?

Actual gut-wrenching reality didn't register immediately.

Then it did, along with the physical reaction, but still no tears.

I kept wondering, as though observing the

scene from a distance, dispassionately, why no tears?

It seemed agonizingly painful for her to tell me. She couldn't right away. It took almost a week for her to work up to it.

She was short-tempered the night she returned after spending four days with two female friends and their three children at our mountain cabin.

Her sentences were short and sharp, almost like headlines rather than her normal, newsy communications, when she called me at my office to say she was home.

I assumed she was simply tired after the drive or perhaps her nerves were frayed from being closeted for four days in our small cabin with the women and their kids.

I was weary and a little depressed as well, having had several unusually-pressure-filled days at the office and feeling deprived by her extended absence.

I stopped for a sandwich on the way home, more to delay our meeting in the hope that she would be in a better mood when I arrived than because I was hungry. I also figured the extra time might help me to prepare to deal with whatever she needed if she was not.

She was still touchy when I arrived.

I recall, in retrospect, that I thought I would have been better off lingering longer, perhaps even stopping off for a couple of drinks before heading home.

As we lay in bed that night, she talked at length about how distressed she was about the cavalier attitude her female companions had about the sanctity of marriage and their own marital relations.

The women -- one a wealthy Washington socialite who had just separated from her husband; the other a several times unhappily-married middle aged matron embittered by her diminishing chances of attracting yet another spouse to support her -- were "out of my league" she said several times.

When I pressed her for an explanation she said, "They just know so much more than I do. They've had so much more experience. I've never even considered some of the stuff they seem to take for granted."

She said they constantly castigated their former or current husbands and saw nothing wrong with having extramarital affairs, dwelling on those topics during their long weekend conversations and making no effort to keep their young children from hearing such talk.

Worse still, she said they laughed at her, saying she was deluding herself when she claimed I wasn't like their husbands and that we were not only faithful to one another but happy as well.

She said she didn't argue with her friends or try to make a case for her own beliefs because they seemed so much more worldly and knowledgeable.

She said she was surprised to hear their opinions and felt trapped and uncomfortable cooped up in the cabin with them, but since they were her guests she couldn't leave. The fact that it rained all weekend, preventing her from even a brief escape for a solitary stroll through the surrounding forest, exacerbated her discomfort.

Her distress appeared to worsen over the next two days at home.

Several times before I left for work in the morning and after I returned in the evening, I found her sitting by the picture window overlooking our backyard, her cheeks wet with tears.

"It's nothing," or "I just don't know," she responded each time I urged her to tell me why she was so upset and how I could help.

Increasingly concerned, I suggested she see a doctor, but she claimed she wasn't sick and really didn't feel that bad.

On the third day my mood began to waver between concern and aggravation.

I was under substantial stress at the office and needed support at home rather than what was becoming a growing burden. I felt I had been sympathetic, offered to help repeatedly, and would have been delighted to provide a solution if she would simply tell me what was bothering her, but I wanted this problem solved immediately.

Her refusal to divulge the reason for her distress, no matter how often I urged, was becoming intolerable.

That Saturday morning the weather cleared into one of those breathtaking Indian-summer days that prompted any able-bodied human to bound outdoors to caress every moment of it knowing, with sublimated sadness, that it might be the last such glorious day before the rapidly approaching chill of winter.

Savoring such a day, luxuriating in the sunshine, would make her problems evaporate like water on a hot griddle, at least that was my theory. I wanted to share the day with her to recapture our usual easy camaraderie now being destroyed by her debilitating depression.

I arose early and carefully carried the orange juice, coffee, toast and her favorite homemade fig preserves I had prepared and arranged artfully on a tray to her bedside, then urged her to eat quickly so we could get out and share this sunshiny day, but she simply rolled over, insisting that she wasn't hungry and wanted to stay in bed.

Exasperated and unable to conceal my disappointment, I told her I would take our seven-year-old son for a motorcycle ride but I expected her to be ready to join us when we returned in two hours since I was sure that being in the sun would brighten her spirits.

Then she suddenly burst into tears and begged me not to make her go out.

I demanded to know her problem.

She said she couldn't tell me.

Incensed, I told her to either see a doctor or pull herself together and be ready to join us, then stalked out to the garage where our son was waiting.

Just as I mounted the bike, she rushed out, tugged on my shirt, and, tears streaming down her cheeks, pleaded with me not to make her leave the house.

I urged her again to tell me about her problem.

Again, she said she couldn't.

Then I demanded that she tell me immediately, insisting that nothing was as bad as it seemed; that putting it off was simply making matters worse; that I could handle anything she had to say, and everything would be alright.

That's when, sobbing and pulling me back toward the house out of earshot of our boy, she finally told me.

"I've been with another man," she said, whimpering as she added, "That's worse than you thought, isn't it?"

Yes. It was considerably worse. This possibility never occurred to me, and I couldn't get my mind around it right away, couldn't make sense of her unexpected disclosure.

When the shock subsided, questions spewed from my mouth with no forethought, no calculation.

"When did it happen? How? Where? Why? Who was he?" all asked in a staccato rant as though I was interviewing a malevolent stranger, with whom I had no connection and an abundance of contempt.

I was aware that something horrible had happened, but my mind once more seemed to stand aside, viewing the scene unemotionally while wondering when I might feel the full impact of her confession.

She said it had happened while she was at our cabin, but she "just couldn't talk about it anymore right now."

Then she became calm, almost comatose, avoiding my eyes, and staring down at some spot on the ground in front of her.

I walked away wondering if she might misconstrue my words and actions; that because I responded to her disclosure without the fury she must have anticipated, but almost academically with questions, this might not be a major crisis.

Shuffling slowly back to the garage I tried to coax the full, miserable meaning of her words into my consciousness so I could deal with it… or at least determine if I could deal with it.

Slowly, like sinking in quicksand, the reality of those words engulfed me while I walked. My wife had made love to another man! She had screwed somebody else! She had fucked some Goddamned asshole! Jesus! Why in Hell had she done it? Where had I gone wrong?

It got worse.

I could see them together; could imagine her kissing some son of a bitch while starting to disrobe in that easy, erotic way she did in our bedroom… my faithful, pure, sweet, fucking wife! Miss Purity! Miss Kindness! My ass!

There she was I imagined, slipping seductively out of her panties; spreading her shapely legs, baring her flat, white, flawless stomach, her delicious mound of jet-black pubic hair shouting for some bastard to mount her; helping him guide his penis into her, loving it! MY WIFE for Christ's sake!

I wanted to scream… to jump up and smash myself to the ground… to run into a tree… to crush myself!

But I didn't.

What I did was walk back to the garage without turning, hoping she was no longer there since I couldn't handle seeing her again right now and wondered if I ever could.

My boy was still standing beside the motorcycle when I arrived, climbed on the bike, helped him up behind me, then cranked it up and sped away.

My mind began to fog over as I drove, blotting out the agonizing pictures it had conjured up, and through some inexplicable miracle of self-preservation I started feeling uncomfortably ambivalent.

Perhaps I should go back and talk to her. She must be miserable not knowing if I would return, and if I did, whether I would maybe beat her before walking away and leaving her forever. Perhaps I should go back and reassure her.

Then I thought I was an idiot for worrying about her. Look at what she had done for God's sake! I should be trying to think of ways to make her suffer, to make her pay for her transgression or to somehow get even.

Then I worried about whether I really felt bad enough, considering the magnitude of what had happened.

Shouldn't I be driving the motorcycle full speed into an oncoming car, or into the river… or something? Why was I sitting here, calmly considering these possibilities instead of just doing it?

Then I thought of my son and how I should be spending this beautiful day with him, making it a joyous one for him to remember… a day I shouldn't spoil for him.

At the same time, I wondered how I could consider such mundane stuff at this moment. Perhaps I should just drop him off near the house and tell him to go home. He would understand one day when I explained why I had done it.

Instead, I drove to a park where he could play while I forced myself to once more confront the ugliness of my wife's revelation.

I had to visualize the horror and all the accompanying agony immediately so I wouldn't sublimate it to avoid the pain and make it impossible to ever purge it from my psyche.

While my son dashed to the nearby swings, I tried to picture the event as it happened, but whenever the painful picture started to come into focus he came running back to me with a question or to point out a bird or a tree and the vision evaporated. I couldn't concentrate with a seven-year-old buzzing about, and this upset me as well.

I wanted to get it out, to see it, grapple with it, wrestle it to the ground and inflict all the pain possible upon myself, hoping to emerge whole after the brutal battle, assuming I survived.

But I couldn't hurt the boy. None of this was his fault.

That made me bitter on a more superficial level -- bitter with her for having ruined what would otherwise have been a beautiful day.

These feelings became interspersed with fragmentary thoughts about the injustice of what she had done and how it could possibly have happened.

Why couldn't she screw someone here and let me catch them at it? Maybe I could have shoved them both down the stairs. Or maybe I would just shoot the man, or my wife, or maybe just beat them both. Then it would be over, and I wouldn't have to think about it any more.

Other, more lurid possibilities also crossed my mind, like slicing off his penis as she watched. That should provide permanent "justice!"

While feeling queasy and a bit embarrassed by such sadistic thoughts, they were inescapable.

After considering the options, I realized I had no idea what I would do but was convinced that a confrontation, whatever the result, would have been more satisfying than the scenario I was given.

Then it occurred to me that maybe I was fortunate. After all, she had confessed her infidelity. She didn't have to. I would never have known. And she suffered visibly because of her action, apparently unable to live with the dirty secret. Some women could have done it and never confessed or suffered guilt at all.

Those "worldly" women she had been with at our cabin would have kept such a secret with little or no remorse. Perhaps that would have been better. Then I wouldn't know and wouldn't be suffering now.

What was I saying? Would I prefer being married to someone who didn't care enough about me to suffer such unbearable pain that she was compelled to confess her infidelity?

Now I began worrying again about how distressed she must be sitting all alone and how I could comfort her.

It was late afternoon when we started home. On the way I wondered what I would say to her, whether I could look at her, whether I'd ever be able to look at her, ever touch her, ever kiss her again. Would we ever be able to make love?

Maybe I should start sleeping in a separate bedroom, but that might drive her to the arms of another man. I'd be miserable knowing she was screwing someone else but would be unable to argue that it wasn't justified.

I wondered if she had told her friends at the cabin, then became angry at myself for wondering, for worrying about what other people might think of me for having been cuckolded.

Who gave a shit? This was far more important than my reputation. This was the worst thing I had ever experienced. This was going to change my life!

Then another slimy thought slithered into my consciousness. What if she became pregnant?

We had been trying for so long to have another baby. What if she had one now? Would I ever be able to look at the child without wondering if it was really mine? And if it wasn't, would I be able to love it? I decided that if she was pregnant, I would take care of her until she gave birth, then tell her to leave and take the child with her.

I grimaced, thinking this was beginning to sound like a bad imitation of a Tennessee Williams tale.

But it wasn't. It was bad reality. My life had been fucked over... literally.

Then I thought: "What's the big deal? Everybody's doing it. It doesn't seem to bother any of the people who talk about it. Some of them even brag about their infidelity and their 'open' marriages. I should feel lucky my wife felt guilty enough to confess."

But what if after having done it once, it became easier to do again, and easier yet the next time. And after the pain her confession caused, she might keep future indiscretions a secret. And even if she were forever faithful, would I believe she was? And if I didn't, wouldn't this drive her to promiscuity?

Would I ever be able to see her dance with another man without wondering if she was sleeping with him, or planning to? Would I ever be comfortable enough to let her make another trip without me, or even be out of my sight? When she was with me would I watch her constantly for any telltale sign that a lover was near. Would I stare at every man, wondering if it was him? And if I did, would I drive myself insane and her away?

Why the hell did she do this to me? What had I done to deserve it?

We tried to avoid one another when I returned home, busying ourselves by pretending to read or watch the news on TV until I tucked the boy in bed and we were finally alone.

We sat in silence at the small table in the breakfast room. Tears welled in her eyes, sporadically springing free to trickle down her cheeks. I felt numb, sitting like a zombie, before finally initiating the conversation by relating, seemingly dispassionately, my concern about her possible pregnancy.

She said if she was pregnant, she would have an abortion. I knew this was either an overt lie or she was deluding herself, since she had wanted another child desperately. In either event I decided it was immaterial since I would follow my earlier decision to care for her until the baby came and then send them away.

Now that the silence was broken, I pressed for details of the event, telling myself that if I could visualize it exactly as it happened, I could confront it and then let it go.

But ultimately, I catered to her discomfort,

demanding no more information than she volunteered, fearing that if I insisted on more at this moment, all communication might dissolve into tears.

Led by soft, empathetic questions delivered in a monotone voice, she responded haltingly, with general descriptions as opposed to the details I desperately desired.

Her girlfriends' constant talk about miserable marriages, infidelity and casual sex depressed her and to escape their company she left the cabin early one morning, before the others had awakened, and drove to a nearby town where she found a coffee shop and sat at a small table sipping hot tea while wondering what she could do to shake her debilitating depression.

Almost immediately, she said a young man came over and asked if he could sit with her, saying he could see her sadness and was a good listener if she cared to talk.

He seemed kind and after a second cup of tea she agreed to his suggestion that a drive in the fresh morning air might cheer her up.

Without giving it further thought, she handed him the keys to her car, and he drove toward the rolling hills outside town.

Sensing something ominous, she said she soon

wished she had not agreed to the drive with this stranger and desperately wanted to return to the cabin.

When she asked him to return to the coffee shop, he instead turned down a dirt road and abruptly veered off to park behind an abandoned barn where he ordered her to take her pants off.

She said she pulled them down and had just got one leg out when he mounted her, forcing his body between her knees as she pressed back against the seat, her eyes squeezed shut, and quickly had his way.

It was over almost before it began, she said, while admitting she never attempted to stop it, somehow becoming resigned to being abused, and was afraid he would hurt her more if she resisted, but she wasn't sure.

When it was done, he drove back to the coffee shop, got out of the car and walked away without saying a word.

She said she never considered reporting the attack though she thought about telling her friends about her ordeal when she returned to the cabin and decided against it.

That was all she would say for now… except that she wanted to be held.

I held her.

Then she said she wanted to be kissed, but I couldn't bring myself to do that even though, with her eyes still tearing, she said she loved me more than ever.

Deep down, I think she wanted to be punished… felt she should be punished and believed punishment would serve as penance, absolving her of the guilt she felt.

A part of me wanted to accommodate her but I couldn't. I'm not sure whether it was because I loved her too much, felt she had already suffered enough, or thought slapping her, or whatever, seemed too small a penalty for her to pay. Besides, the idea of physically abusing any woman had always been onerous to me.

Then I remembered that as a child, once I got spanked for something, my slate was clean, like I imagined Confession must be for Catholics.

The spanking and subsequent absolution was far easier to deal with than the lectures I received from my mother as a teenager, when I was too big to spank. When I did something wrong at that time, she'd say: "If you loved me, you wouldn't do that," and I carried the guilt around for weeks, sometimes longer. Some of it may still be lingering somewhere down in the depths of my subconscious now that mother has gone.

I also considered the possibility that because

my wife had learned I wasn't going to beat her, leave her, or throw her out, she might think she had worried needlessly. It had been so easy that maybe the next time she wouldn't worry about the consequences since there were none.

The thought that she had now unburdened herself, and in doing so had placed the burden on me, was discomfiting. It was she who had done this thing, but she had eliminated her guilt by confessing. Now she was comfortable. It was I who had to live with it.

Then came the recurring thought that this was better than not telling me since keeping it a secret might lead to another secret, and another, and another.

"Crap," I muttered.

That night we sat up late watching TV.

A casual observer might have thought it was just another Saturday night for a dull couple with nothing better to do and nothing on their minds.

I glanced at her frequently and was reminded how very pretty and sweetly pure she seemed but felt like vomiting when I was bludgeoned again by the thought of her screwing her ass off in the front seat of the car with a stranger.

Mercifully, the thought seemed to pass more quickly now.

When we could stay awake no longer, we started awkwardly up the stairs toward the bedroom. Once reaching the top, she stopped and attempted to kiss me, but I still couldn't.

If I did, everything would seem alright, as if nothing had happened, and everything wasn't alright, and something had happened.

I started to sleep in the guest bedroom, then decided not to and crawled into our oversized bed, scrunching down near the far edge on my side for a long while, thinking about her being with someone else.

Maybe, I thought, instead of never touching her I should screw her hard, venting my anger by ravaging her with brutal sex. I was surprised, distressed and bemused by the fact that such thoughts caused me to become sexually aroused.

That's when I decided that since I would eventually make love to her again anyway, I might as well get it over with right now. I rolled over, kissed her on the ear and, when she responded, mounted her without uttering my usual loving words or indulging in our normal, long-lingering foreplay.

She seemed unusually excited and reached a climax after only a few moments of unusually powerful gyrations. Then she hugged me and said she loved me more than anything in the world.

After sliding to my side of the bed again I lay there for a long time wondering if hers had been genuine sexual fulfillment or just relief at finding I could still make love to her.

While her wild abandon was exciting, it seemed somehow unseemly. How could she allow herself to be so wanton so soon after what she had done? A fleeting vision of her being mounted on the car seat flickered across my mind, and the budding thought of a second round of love-making dissipated rapidly, along with my lingering erection.

The next day was Sunday. She sat beside me, knitting a sweater for her father while I watched football on TV.

"It's like nothing happened," I thought, watching her concentrate on her work.

It seems easier each day now to suppress those painful images when they try to invade my consciousness. It's almost as if it was all just a bad dream.

Home Sweet Home

"I'm sorry about Nanna. I tried to help. I really thought she'd be alright after a while. Maybe if I had been with her all the time… if I wasn't in school. Anyway Helen, I'm sorry."

John spoke to his mother's profile as she slowly shifted the old Chevrolet's gears, coaxing it through the massive iron gates of the asylum.

He had started to say "Mother" rather than "Helen," but it felt too awkward. He had never known her as his mother. She had been Helen for as long as he could remember.

Nanna, his grandmother, had been his mother for the last 12 years, and he could hardly recall the first three, having tried for so long to forget them.

He had pretty much succeeded.

John's recollection of the incessant bickering between Helen and his father had finally softened into the formless fog of semi-forgotten unpleasantness.

Things would be different now. Nanna and Poppa were both gone, and Helen was to be his mother again.

He wondered if he could ever call her that without feeling self-conscious. No, John decided, it would have to be Helen, even though he'd be living with her now.

Besides, he thought, viewing her tiny frame sitting rigidly upright so she could see over the steering wheel, Helen didn't look as though she should be anyone's mother.

She was so small, so young and, yes, so very pretty, he thought.

Soft, honey-colored hair caressed the side of her face, partially hiding the upturned nose and almost too-full lips which, together with the profusion of freckles, gave her a perennial schoolgirl look.

He wriggled around, trying to seem nonchalant while shifting his position to scrutinize Helen more closely.

Actually, he thought, slowly releasing the air filling his lungs like a balloon nearing its bursting point, she's absolutely beautiful.

How old would she be now, he wondered, thinking they might pass for siblings or even, maybe, sweethearts... almost.

"She was barely 14 when I was born," he

mused, recalling Nanna and Poppa's kitchen conversations he had heard late at night while hunkering down in hiding at the head of the stairs.

That's a year younger than he was now. That would make her 28 or 29, but she certainly didn't look that old, he thought, still savoring the sight of her.

John wondered what she had done all those years.

He had heard she put up with his father's drinking and abuse for almost three years before their divorce and then how, unable to support her son, she was finally forced to leave him with her parents.

He knew she lived in a rooming house and worked as a secretary at the gas company in Savannah, where they were heading now, but that's about all he knew about this woman who was his mother.

Savannah was 200 miles east of Thomasville, a small town known mostly for its furniture factories, situated in the sparsely populated southwest corner of Georgia where he had lived with his grandparents.

John never understood why Helen had waited so long to visit him that first time four years ago.

He was too engrossed with his own feelings

of rejection to consider that she was barely more than a child herself when she left him, armed with only a junior-high-school education; burdened by deep psychological wounds from an abusive marriage; and mired in her own time-swallowing struggle to simply survive.

He couldn't know that when she finally achieved sufficient stability to visit, guilt over having abandoned him dampened her spirit, and diminished her inclination.

John mistook her failure to provide input regarding his upbringing for disinterest when, in reality, she felt she had no right to interfere after having abdicated her parental responsibility to his grandparents.

Their conversations during her subsequent monthly visits were chatty and pleasant, but mostly centered on his current interests and activities. Neither his nor her past or future problems and plans were ever discussed.

Now, here they were, mother and son, virtual strangers on a new life's journey to who knew where.

"I know you tried," she said, interrupting her own troubled thoughts to answer her son. "You did just fine. Nobody could have done more. Nanna simply gave up when Poppa passed."

"Well, don't worry," replied John, trying to reciprocate his mother's reassurance. "Everything will be alright. They'll take good care of Nanna."

"Of course they will Harv… John," she stumbled, almost calling him Harvey, her former husband's name, a name she hadn't spoken for years.

They do look alike, she thought, and he seems more like a man than a boy for his age. Can he only be 15?

Here he is, trying to comfort me when Poppa, the only father he's ever known, died of a stroke just two months ago, and now Nanna's mind has gone.

And he's so big -- big as Harvey ever was -- and, yes, just as handsome, she thought with conscious pride, glancing intermittently at her son as she drove, secretly admiring his thick, curly hair and muscular arms.

She had heard John already needed to shave every other day to rid his face of still soft but ever thickening whiskers.

"I'm afraid I, we, don't have very much space but we'll make out alright until I can afford something better," said Helen.

Then, unable to resist a lengthy yawn, she covered her mouth with the back of her right hand and added: "I need to stop for some coffee. I can hardly keep my eyes open."

They had been driving for almost two hours when she pulled to the curb in front of an innocuous-looking restaurant in one of those equally innocuous-looking crossroad towns that freckle the face of Georgia.

"I'll drive if you're tired," John offered. "I'm a good driver. Poppa always told me that. He used to let me drive for him all the time."

"Thanks, but it's OK, I'll be fine after I have a cup of coffee," Helen replied.

Once inside the cafe, they sat down at a long, stool-lined counter, ordering coffee and doughnuts from the plump woman wearing a red-and-white checkered apron whose attention they had diverted from the movie magazine she was hunched over at the far end of the counter when they entered.

They remained silent as the woman, who wore a motionless, mask-like frown while taking and serving their order, waddled back to her stool to refocus on the magazine, imagining herself a movie star, just as she did when she was a high school cheerleader 40 years and 45 pounds earlier.

Between sips of coffee, Helen chattered nervously. "There's a good high school just four blocks from the boarding house. It's got the city's best baseball and basketball teams. You'll love it. I know you'll make lots of friends. And there's Ben. You'll like Ben. He's so friendly and helpful."

"Who's Ben?" John interrupted.

"Benjamin Roberts, but you can just call him Ben. Everybody does. Ben lives in the house with us, but he's kind of a handyman. He knows everything about fixing things. He's strong as an ox but really gentle, and he'll do anything for you. He's always kind of dirty but that's because he spends most of his time crawling around and under things working with his hands. Anyway, we're like a family."

"Family?" questioned John, his eyes furrowing.

"Well, that's what it feels like anyway. There's only three of us… four now with you, John. Mrs. Creech is the landlady, but she's really like an older sister, except she's so prim and proper. She's a real southern lady!"

After finishing their coffee, John reached for the check before Helen could pick it up.

"I've got this," he said. "I had a newspaper route in Thomasville and saved some money. Do you think I could get a paper route in Savannah?"

Helen said her boss knew lots of people at the

newspaper and she was confident he could convince them to hire him.

That brief conversation melted their years of separation. A feeling of camaraderie covered them like a cozy blanket during the last 80 miles of the trip.

Only sporadic observations about an erratic driver or unusual road sign were made as they sat in silence, each reflecting on their uncertain future, while still surreptitiously stealing glances at one another, smiling self-consciously when they were caught.

It was just after 10 p.m. when Helen slowed the car to negotiate the hairpin turn three blocks from her boarding house.

"If you're ever driving, be very careful going around this curve," she cautioned. "It's treacherous. There are two or three bad wrecks here every month."

Moments later, they pulled into the wide driveway beside a two-story, white, wood-framed house on East 39th Street, just off of Drayton.

Ben, barefooted and bare-chested, donned in dirty khaki trousers on this hot, humid evening, was beside Helen's door almost before she stopped the car.

John watched the burly man bend to open her

door. His muscles tensed as he spotted Ben staring at Helen's thighs when her thin cotton dress slid high as she swung her legs around to get out.

"Welcome home, Miss Helen, we shore missed you," he said, speaking in a slurred southern drawl through a grin that revealed yellow, misshapen teeth.

"And Mr. John! I shore looked forward to meetin' you," he continued, holding out a ham-sized hand to the boy when he walked around the car.

"Ya'll go on in and git comfortable while I git these little bags," he said, eying John's three suitcases on the back seat.

"I can get my bags," said John, surprising even himself with his brusque reply.

"Wull, alright, whatever you want," Ben mumbled, backing away like a hurt puppy, causing John to feel a momentary twinge of guilt for having been so curt to someone who was offering him a helping hand.

The ensuing, awkward silence was shattered by Mrs. Creech when she trotted up to the trio with a squeal of delight, wrapping her arms around Helen and kissing her before stepping back, grasping Helen's small hands with her own long, thin fingers, while gazing down at her saying softly: "Welcome home, my dear."

John thought his mother seemed slightly flustered, like he did that time when he discovered his fly was unzipped when he came to the dinner table back in Thomasville, before she turned to say, "This is our landlady, Mrs. Creech. Mrs. Creech, my son, John."

Mrs. Creech was 50ish, with short, iron-gray hair combed back in what would have been considered a duck tail were she a man. She was wiry thin, with wide shoulders accentuated by the padding in her blouse and her narrow, boyish hips. At 5 feet, 11 inches, she was slightly taller than John.

"Hello Johnny," she said, smiling as she extended her hand in greeting. "My, you're a big fellow, aren't you? I didn't expect you would be so big! And aren't you a handsome lad."

"Let's go inside and make some coffee while the boys bring in the bags," she continued, grasping Helen's hand and leading her into the house without waiting for an answer, leaving John alone with Ben.

Relenting as he strained to heft two of the heavy suitcases from the rear seat, John said, "I think I'll take you up on your offer, Ben. I'll take these two if you'll grab the other one."

Trudging toward the house, with John weaving unsteadily under the weight of his luggage, they climbed the three steps on the stairs to the wide front porch, crossed it and entered the house through a screened door which was swiftly pulled shut by a single, snake-like spring.

A short hallway opened into a massive, rectangular space which served as a combination communal living/sitting/dining room. In better times it was the parlor of the huge old two-story house, the second floor of which had been closed off and was now unused.

Four doors, two on each of the long side walls, were spaced evenly with those on the left leading to the separate bedrooms and baths of Mrs. Creech and Ben, while the first on the right led to Helen's bedroom and bath. The other one on that side opened into a large kitchen and breakfast room.

A huge oval oriental rug with a massive mahogany dining table surrounded by matching ladderback chairs squatting in its center covered most of the polished oak floor, while small throw rugs were scattered around its circumference.

Overstuffed leather and fabric-covered furniture, including a pair of wingback chairs, two long sofas and several rockers were sprinkled randomly around.

John noticed a yellow line of light under Mrs. Creech's door before Ben led him into Helen's room.

"Well, this'll be it," said Ben, flipping on the overhead light as John squeezed past him, to slide his big bags inside.

The bedroom was a perfect square, 20 feet to a side, with a pair of windows looking out over the side yard on the wall opposite the door. The pull-down shades covering the windows puffed inward when the door opened, sucking a warm breeze laden with the sweet scent of Confederate jasmine through the room.

John placed his suitcases on the metal day bed beneath the windows, momentarily mesmerized by the intoxicating aroma before forcing himself to focus on his surroundings.

A wide, ornately-carved, wood dressing table with a massive mirror was centered on the wall to the right of the entrance. Hinged extensions of the main mirror hugged the edges of the table, to the right of which was a door opening into a spacious closet.

A white metal double bed covered with a cotton spread sprinkled with replicas of yellow daffodils dominated the room.

Its heavy headboard pressed against the wall to the left, and a door beside it opened into a large bathroom, with a black-and-white tiled floor.

The bathroom contained a plain white American Standard toilet and matching pedestal sink with a mirrored metal medicine cabinet above it.

A small scale with peeling white paint sat forlornly on the floor between them while a massive white porcelain bathtub was squeezed into an alcove to the right, squatting on short, bowed legs atop claw feet clutching spheres the size of billiard balls.

Leaving his suitcases on the day bed, John turned to follow Ben into the living room where Helen and Mrs. Creech stood smoothing their hair, studiously avoiding eye contact.

Ben made an odd guttural sound deep in his throat when he saw them and at that precise moment, the wind shifted, blowing open the door under which John had seen the light and filling the room with the noxious odor of rotten eggs, made the more odious by the sweet scent which preceded it.

The scene, the sound and the smell converged, causing John's skin to crawl.

"What's that smell?" he asked, grimacing.

"Oh, that's the smell from the paper mill down on the river," answered Helen. "It only happens when the wind blows from the north, which it seldom does.

"You'll get used to it after a while. We hardly

notice it anymore. Folks in Savannah call it the smell of money because the mill is the biggest employer in the area."

"Well, I guess we'd better start fixing that coffee," said Mrs. Creech. "I'll bet you could use some about now. And you must be worn down from your long day, Johnny. Why don't you and Ben relax and watch some television while we prepare the coffee?

"Come along Helen, I can use your help."

John wondered why they hadn't already started the coffee, in view of Mrs. Creech's earlier rush from the car to make it, and why she needed help with such a simple undertaking.

He considered discussing these thoughts with Ben but decided against it, scrunching down instead in a corner of the big leather sofa facing the TV, feeling very much alone.

Fifteen minutes and five commercials later Helen and Mrs. Creech emerged from the kitchen with a large silver tray containing a coffee pot, an antique silver sugar-and-cream set with matching silver spoons, and four delicate cups and saucers which she placed on the big table.

"Forgive me Johnny, would you prefer milk or a Coke?" asked Mrs. Creech, causing Helen to squirm in her chair almost imperceptibly with a twinge of guilt for not having been so solicitous of her own son.

"No thanks, this is fine, I drink coffee all the time at home… er, I mean I'm used to coffee," John replied, trying to assert his maturity but stumbling over the as yet unassimilated fact that this was now his home.

After coffee, the quartet watched two TV sitcoms, both summer re-runs of programs which would be replaced by similarly mediocre fare the following season.

Then Helen stretched, announced that she had to get to bed in order to be up in time for work the next day, and told John he could stay up for a while if he wanted since he could sleep late.

Her son quickly declined, saying he was tired and needed to hit the sack as well, though in truth he wanted to avoid sitting alone with Ben and Mrs. Creech. They were Helen's friends, and he was trying to be pleasant but something about them made him uncomfortable.

"You go ahead and take your bath first," directed Helen after they entered their room. "I'll make your bed and brush my hair while you do. You'll find a clean washcloth and towels on the rack by the tub."

John hesitated, looking down at his feet before

blurting: "I don't have any pajamas. I sleep in my underwear!"

Helen smiled reassuringly, saying, "That's alright, after all…" she had started to say "I'm your mother," but added instead "don't most men? I know your father always did."

John's embarrassment was immediately transformed into a feeling of chest-expanding pride when he heard Helen classify him with "men", and though she was not conscious of it, that's how Helen thought of him. It was John's rare display of naive awkwardness, the only times he exhibited his true age, that surprised her.

When he emerged from the bathroom wearing jockey shorts, she had already turned down his bed and unpacked his clothes, but the results of those efficient efforts escaped his notice.

His eyes were drawn to Helen, who was seated on a bench facing the dressing table mirror brushing the long, lush hair hanging soft and loose over her shoulders, down to the middle of her back.

She was wearing a sheer white negligee beneath which her skimpy pink panties were clearly visible.

John lay on the day bed, propping himself up on a pillow, arms behind his head, while he watched.

Neither spoke as she continued brushing her hair, counting in a whisper to the 200 brush strokes of her nightly routine.

With each stroke, Helen pulled her hair over her shoulder, exposing her delicate neck and occasionally causing the sleeve of her negligee to slip down her arm, forcing her to interrupt her rhythmic stroking to pull it back in place.

Unbeknownst to her, each time it slipped John had a brief but breathtaking glimpse of the edge of the perfect pink aureola surrounding the nipple of her left breast prompting an unaccustomed stirring to slither slowly through his groin stretching his jockey shorts tight with his stiffening manhood.

That manhood grew uncontrollably with each glimpse forcing him to roll over onto his stomach to hide his excitement. Still, unable to resist, he squirmed into a position where he could prop the side of his head atop his pillow to continue watching.

Rock hard, he tightened his buttocks, slowly pressing his body deep into the mattress, prompting a painfully pleasant sensation similar to the feeling he experienced stroking himself behind the locked bathroom door at his grandmother's house while running water full force in the sink to obliterate the telltale slapping sound.

But watching Helen's rhythmic movement caused a different, somehow more exciting sensation than masturbating while staring at a barren bathroom floor.

"Two hundred," Helen sighed, before rising and stopping briefly beside his bed to pat his head on her way to the bathroom. She had started to pat his firm bottom but altered her target after seeing the curly black hair covering his legs thicken where it disappeared beneath his shorts.

A tingling sensation tip toed down her back and along the inside of her thighs as she withdrew her hand and said, "Goodnight," her husky voice soft as silk.

"Night," said John into his pillow, afraid to turn over before she left the room.

Helen treated herself to a leisurely, steaming hot bath, leaning back against the big tub's gentle slope softly washing her body while watching with casual curiosity as soap bubbles slid slowly over and between her firm breasts.

She was pleased with her body and had every right to be. It was as tight as a teenager's but filled with the pulsating ripeness of a mature woman.

Helen often wondered how Harvey could have sacrificed such assets to become a philanderer, chasing older and less attractive women during his frequent drunken escapades.

Perhaps he didn't think she would leave him, confident in his belief that she couldn't survive on her own and that her sensuous body could never deprive itself of the pleasure he provided.

Maybe he figured he could have it all, controlling Helen's delicious, willing but innocent body while at the same time bedding down with the town's sexually experienced harlots who were happy to do anything he asked.

That assumption was close to the mark.

God knows it had been difficult for her to forgo the pleasures to which he had introduced her. She relished his sometimes rough, always knowledgeable lovemaking, staying awake many nights to savor the memory of those sensations long after Harvey had gone to sleep.

Still, deep in some dark corner of her mind, she knew it wasn't just her husband. It was sexual activity itself that she cherished.

Helen pressed the palms of her hands hard against the mound of hair between her legs and started fingering the taut pinkness below.

She was breathing rapidly before becoming fully conscious of what she was doing. Startled and chagrined, she struggled to her feet, slipping before frantically catching herself on the side of the tub in her haste to spray cold shower water over her body, forgetting she wasn't wearing a shower cap.

That didn't matter now. All that mattered was that she had to subdue the almost irresistible desire gripping her body.

Meanwhile, John was losing a brief struggle with his own willpower. It started just after Helen closed the bathroom door. That's when he began trying to imagine exactly what she was doing.

Was she already nude, he wondered. Maybe she was leaning over to slip out of those pink panties. What would she look like underneath?

"She's your mother, you bastard!" he muttered, cursing himself for his carnal thoughts.

Then he heard bathwater running and visualized Helen stepping over the side of the tub, exposing the pinkness between her legs before slowly slipping down in the water's warm embrace as it rose up her thighs while she lay back, her arms resting atop the tub's rounded sides.

Maybe the hot water made her perspire, causing little droplets to caress her breasts, dripping like nectar from her delicious nipples.

"Jesus," he muttered, squeezing the bulge in his shorts, then reaching inside to grasp the offending organ with both hands, yanking it hard in a desperate effort to obliterate these thoughts.

Sweat soaked his forehead as erotic sensation was replaced by excruciating pain when he rolled over rapidly just as Helen emerged from the bathroom. He grimaced in silence, pretending to be asleep while she laid out her clothes for the next day before crawling into bed.

Just after turning off her bedside lamp, Helen whispered: "Goodnight, John."

He clinched his fists but did not answer.

Each of them wrestled with worrisome thoughts before finally falling into uneasy sleep.

John also feigned sleep the following morning, keeping his eyes closed and his head turned toward the wall while Helen dressed and departed, but the moment he heard her car start he jumped up, made his bed, dressed and hastened from the house to avoid seeing either Mrs. Creech or Ben.

He spent the day wandering around the neighborhood, exploring in ever widening circles to familiarize himself with his new surroundings while pushing his body toward exhaustion to expunge the lingering guilt from his previous night's thoughts.

Helen attempted to blot out similar memories by immersing herself in work all day, not even bothering to take a lunch break.

Neither was notably successful.

Mrs. Creech was putting the final touches on the dinner table, laying silver out in precise order on linen napkins beside the colorful summer dishes she had carefully arranged on an heirloom tablecloth when the two arrived at the house simultaneously.

A dozen white gardenias floated on the surface of the water in a shallow crystal bowl in the center of the table, their intoxicating aroma floating in the air.

The scene and the scent provided a perfect setting for a summer evening in the south.

Even Ben, scrubbed clean and wearing a freshly ironed white shirt and khaki trousers, seemed shiny.

After inviting the trio to be seated, Mrs. Creech scurried to the kitchen, then emerged with a tray laden with bowls of fresh-caught Georgia shrimp and grits which she had thickened with cheddar cheese and heavy cream, along with side dishes of sliced ripe tomatoes, crisp chilled cucumbers, and a skillet of steaming hot cornbread.

"Your mother tells me this is your favorite meal," she announced, smiling primly at John as she placed the platter on the table. "I wanted to prepare it for you to welcome you to your new home."

"Thank you so much, Mrs. Creech," replied John, mustering a grin. "It looks scrumptious."

Despite the festive atmosphere Mrs. Creech had tried to create, the dinner soon meandered off into silence.

After the meal, the quartet again settled down on the couch to watch television and, after an hour, Helen again departed for the bedroom.

This time John remained with the others, hoping to avoid the previous night's discomfort by staying up until after Helen was asleep.

His good intentions faded rapidly when Mrs. Creech started nervously shifting her position while Ben crouched in the far corner of the couch, staring at both of them through half closed eyelids. When he could tolerate the tension no longer, John claimed he couldn't keep his eyes open and had to go to bed.

Even as he said it he wondered if he was using their annoying actions to justify his urge to be alone with Helen. The looks Mrs. Creech and Ben gave him as he left did nothing to assuage that feeling, but neither did they delay his resolute march toward the bedroom.

Knocking lightly, he thought he heard Helen take a deep breath before opening the door, still buttoning her nightgown as he entered, inadvertently offering him another brief glimpse of her rose-tipped breast before turning away.

"I'll take my bath first tonight," Helen said huskily, hastening toward the bathroom without looking directly at him.

The situation grew worse that night.

The throbbing in John's trousers started almost as soon as he entered the room. He stared at the bathroom door so long it grew fuzzy. The knob seemed to grow exponentially, reaching the size of a watermelon as it beckoned him to grasp it, yank the door open and sample the sweetness inside.

He balled his fists until his fingernails cut into his palms, drawing little crescents of blood as he fought the impulse to turn the knob and hurl himself toward Helen who, he imagined, was standing nude, nipples taut, with arms akimbo, beckoning him.

When he heard her foot splash into the tub water, he could no longer restrain himself. Leaning back against the bathroom door, he masturbated, squeezing his eyes shut as he imagined the unimaginable while holding his breath so Helen wouldn't hear his heavy panting.

John's fantasy, along with his frenzied hand

motion, froze at the sound of a knock on the bedroom door. He stood in pained silence as it came again, this time more insistent, and Helen called out for him to see who was there.

"Yes, who's there?", he spoke toward the door, anxiety turning his voice into a hoarse groan.

"It's me, Mrs. Creech, Johnny. I need to see your mother."

"She's taking a bath," he answered, trying to speak in a normal tone while desperately hoping Mrs. Creech wouldn't ask to come in and wait.

"Tell her to come over and see me when she's finished," Mrs. Creech replied before leaving, much to his relief, without waiting for a response.

John delivered the message through the closed bathroom door before staggering over to the daybed where he huddled until Helen emerged, then got up and moved rapidly into the bathroom.

Once alone, Helen turned back the covers on her bed and lay down, declaring to herself that she would not go to Mrs. Creech.

In the quiet of the room, she could hear John's trousers drop to the floor followed by the splash of water when he climbed into the tub.

She pictured the hair on his legs and the place where it thickened between them.

"But he's my son! He's only a boy," she scolded herself, only to hear a small, insistent voice within her prompting, "But he's a young man. He's kind and handsome and big, and you've never known him as a son."

That prompting turned her thoughts to a vision of his muscular body pressing down on hers as she began writhing, thrusting up to meet him.

"It's been so long… so long," she sighed before slipping silently out of the room to run across the parlor toward Mrs. Creech's door. When she returned, half satisfied and suffering increasingly stifling guilt, she was relieved to see John was sleeping, albeit fitfully.

Their anxiety worsened as the week crawled by like a turtle slowly struggling across a highway in the heat of a mid-summer day.

Each night, with miniscule modifications, became a repetition of the last.

When Helen entered the tub, John faced the bathroom door frantically pulling on his throbbing penis while pressing its swollen head against the keyhole just below the knob, imagining other, more tender and receptive openings he wanted to press against. Just before ejaculation, he grabbed the paper towels he had stashed in the back of his shorts and spewed a stream of thick, opaque semen into the wad.

Muscles quivering, he breathed a relieved sigh, leaned against the door as he wiped himself off, then squeezed the soggy paper into a ball before slipping it into the space between his mattress and the wall to dispose of after Helen departed the next morning.

And now, rather than trying to resist, Helen headed directly to Mrs. Creech's room, her thighs trembling in anticipation, as soon as John started his bath.

Their lingering guilt intensified daily making it almost impossible for mother and son to face one another when they were alone.

Helen found some relief by burying herself in work at her office, but John's days, filled with self-deprecation, were almost as painful as his nights.

Mrs. Creech seemed to grow progressively more jealous of John because he shared Helen's bedroom. When Helen was absent, her questions turned resentful, and he could feel her piercing stare following him around the room.

She seemed bent on making him feel useless and juvenile, constantly referring to him as a little boy, perhaps trying to convince herself of this through repetition.

Ben's fawning attention was almost as bad. He

kept offering to do things for John, acting like a doting father, but one with whom John had nothing in common and toward whom he had no feeling except disgust.

Ben embellished their relationship when he talked to Helen, telling her how much he liked her son and how well they got along. It became obvious and infuriating to John that the slovenly handyman was using him in an effort to gain Helen's affection. He grew more repulsed each time he caught Ben leering at her, and his discomfort was exacerbated because Helen seemed oblivious to Ben's ulterior motives. He was especially distressed because she seemed pleased by what she thought was his growing friendship with Ben.

John started leaving the house early each day to avoid his tormentors, often busying himself tinkering with the old Model-A Ford perched atop blocks beneath the huge oak tree at the far end of the yard where it had been relegated to rust years ago.

The car, like the big house, had belonged to Mrs. Creech's father, and both had seen far better days.

John was convinced that with fresh oil and gas and a new coil, spark plugs and wires, he could breathe life into the old car. It would need new tires and a battery, but he figured he could acquire all of these after he found a job and saved up his money.

Whenever Ben entered the yard, he abandoned his tinkering to wander around the neighborhood. Though his departure was initially to avoid contact with the burly man, he started relishing the solitude along with the warmth of Savannah's early summer.

Two weeks after his arrival, John awakened one morning with a start, realizing he had overslept.

Tormented the previous hot, breezeless night by troubling, erotic thoughts that stuck in his mind like the sweat-soaked sheet stuck to his body, he had been unable to fall asleep until after 4 a.m., and it was already 10 o'clock when he sprang from bed, dressed rapidly, then held the door slightly ajar to peer around the parlor.

Seeing no one there, he headed to the kitchen, resolving to make a fresh effort to improve his deteriorating relationship with Mrs. Creech and Ben.

After all, they were Helen's friends and he had to live with them. He'd try to make the best of the situation by being pleasant and helpful around the house to win them over.

Finding the kitchen empty, he started preparing breakfast, placing three strips of bacon in a big iron frying pan and two slices of wheat bread into the toaster before cracking a pair of big brown eggs into a small mixing bowl.

Adding a dash of milk to the eggs, he stirred the liquid into a light-yellow froth with a fork, planning to pour it into the hot skillet to scramble once the bacon was done, regretting only that he was unable to find any cheese to add to the eggs.

The bacon had just started to sizzle when Mrs. Creech strolled briskly into the room.

"Goodness! What are you doing, child?" she asked, in an exasperated tone that dampened his altruistic resolve.

"I was just fixing breakfast," he responded. "I hope you don't mind. I didn't want to bother anyone. Would you and Ben like some bacon and eggs? I'll be happy to put more on."

"Nonsense," she said, her high-pitched voice frazzling his nerves like fingernails scraping a blackboard. "The kitchen is no place for a boy. Go sit it the parlor while I prepare your breakfast, and from now on, if you want anything, just call me."

John sat quietly while Mrs. Creech finished cooking what he had started, dutifully thanking her when she placed the food before him. He was more relieved than offended when she left abruptly, without acknowledging his courtesy.

The meal was less palatable than he had anticipated, but he finished it quickly and had just begun washing the dishes when Mrs. Creech suddenly appeared again to insist that he stop, saying, "I appreciate your trying to help, but I can't afford to have my good dishes broken by little boys."

"Don't worry, Mrs. Creech," he said. "I'll be very careful. I'm used to doing the dishes at home."

"This is your home Johnny, though you can't seem to remember it," she corrected. "Now go outside and play in the yard. Mind now, don't go out in the street."

Disheartened, John nonetheless made one more attempt at reconciliation asking, "Can I cut your grass or wash the windows or something, Mrs. Creech? I really want to help. I want to do my share."

"That's man's work, Johnny," she replied differentially. "That's what I keep Ben around for. You just go out and play."

John shuffled out, feeling both useless and hopeless.

He was sitting on the front steps trying to decide what to do while waiting for Helen to return from work when Ben rounded the corner of the house.

"How you doin' this morning, Johnny boy?" Ben asked, wiping his greasy hands along the sides of his dirty jeans. "I've been waitin' for ya to get up. Wanted to play a little catch with ya. How bout it, boy?"

"No thanks, Ben," John replied. "I've got some stuff I have to do this morning."

"Don't worry, boy," said Ben. "I won't hurt ya. I'll throw real easy. I just wanna show ya a couple of tricks I know. Show ya how to throw one of them fast balls and maybe a curve. Make ya a big league pitcher!"

"Well that does sound great," John replied with mock enthusiasm, chafing from Ben's aspersion that he might be afraid. "I can put off my plans for those kinds of lessons!"

Ben trotted into the house, then returned immediately with a battered hard ball and two weathered fielder's gloves, directing John to stand with this back to the house then moved over to the edge of the yard about 40 feet away, turned to face John and shouted, "Awright, boy, here ya go," before tossing a soft overhand lob to John.

Calling on his experience as a star pitcher in the Southwest Georgia Junior Boys League the previous year, John whipped back a wide, looping sidearm curve.

Ben figured it was a wild throw and moved left to field it just as the ball broke by him to his right, catching him completely off guard. He watched helplessly as the ball bounced across the street and into the deep weeds on the far side.

Shuffling after it, Ben kicked his way through weeds for several minutes trying to find the ball, minutes during which he grew hot from the searing sun and hotter still from a growing recognition that crawled over him like the sweat soaking his T-shirt, recognition that a smart-assed kid had just made him look stupid.

Grabbing the ball, he turned to hurl it toward John with all his strength. It traveled in an almost level trajectory, whistling as it covered the 80 feet or so from across the street.

Moving with gazelle-like grace, John leaped to his right, catching the missile while swinging his arm back in an easy arc to soften the sting when it hit his glove.

Once his burly adversary was back in position, John took a full, menacing, windmill windup while Ben braced, legs spread and knees slightly bent, anticipating a retaliatory fast ball. Instead, John offered up a deceptively slow-moving knuckle ball which Ben again misjudged. The ball taunted him, plopping down at his feet despite his belated but determined effort to lunge for it.

"Say, boy, you know sumpin' bout pitchin don-cha?" he yelled, leering at his young antagonist before hurling the ball back to him.

"I've tossed a few balls, but I'm always happy to learn from an expert," John countered, smiling as he stretched nonchalantly, then fired his specialty, a sizzling fast ball.

It stung Ben's hand through his poorly padded glove, and, incensed, he hurled it back as hard as he could.

The ball soared ten feet above John's head, with a velocity that almost flattened it against the side of the house, just inches from a window.

"I'd better quit now," John said, breaking the ensuing silence while stifling the urge to laugh.

"No, no, boy, don't quit now," Ben pleaded, after regaining his composure and becoming worried about alienating John and damaging his chances with Helen.

"I was just a little wild, just gettin' warmed up. Let's give 'er another go."

"I can't," said John. "I've got to go down to the newspaper to see about a job. I have to leave now."

"You want me to go with ya?"

"No, I have to handle this by myself."

"Wull, you tell your mama how good I was to ya. Tell her I played ball with ya, awright? You'll do that, huh?"

"I'll tell you honestly, Ben, if I tell Helen anything it will be to stay away from you because you're a dirty old man who's trying to get next to her," John growled.

"Why you little…" Ben muttered, balling his fist as he started towards John before restraining himself once more and saying, "Now don't talk like that, Johnny boy. I don't mean nothin'. I just wanna be friends."

"You better stay away from Helen, or I'll tell her quicker than you think!" John shouted over his shoulder as he headed down the sidewalk.

"Well, what time are you comin' back, Johnny?" Ben called after him. "What should I tell your mamma and Mrs. Creech?"

"Just tell 'em I'll be back in time for supper… by 6 o'clock… that I went downtown," John yelled without breaking his stride.

Although he had made up the newspaper visit as an excuse to get away, he decided he might as well go there now.

John felt better and better about this decision

as he moved, his senses quickening along with his pace, heightened by the soft wind swaying beard-like strands of moss drooping from the ancient oaks standing like wrinkled sentinels along both sides of the street, their branches embracing in the middle, to form a canopy above it.

He interrupted his progress frequently to admire semi-tropical foliage cascading across the city's park-like squares. The sidewalk passed straight through those squares, which the street itself was forced to circumnavigate.

The air was redolent with the scent of Confederate and Carolina jasmine, honeysuckle and gardenias which flourished in the squares and spread through the lush little yards of historic townhomes lining the streets surrounding them, while wisteria, crepe myrtle and lantana painted the area with glorious color.

Most yards sported at least one gigantic magnolia tree decorated with pink or ivory-colored blossoms which reminded him of Christmas tree ornaments.

Although most of the magnificent camellia and azalea blooms for which Savannah was best known had perished by late spring, the picture-book squares still served up a visual feast.

Save for the age of the trees, the squares remained much the same as they had when Gen.

James Oglethorpe designed the city around them 300 years earlier. Even now, when a horse-drawn carriage laden with tourists moseyed around one of them, John felt he was transported back to a slower, sweeter era in the South.

Savannah was indeed a beautiful, sweet-scented city, except on those rare days when the wind blew those foul vapors from the paper mill over it.

The distance from the rooming house to the newspaper on Bay Street was 39 blocks.

John was smiling when he arrived. His smile spread even wider a half hour later when he departed after meeting with the newspaper's circulation manager.

The rotund, red-haired manager agreed to hire him immediately because the regular carrier in John's area was moving to Atlanta with his parents the following week and he desperately needed a replacement.

John felt like he was floating on air. His body seemed to levitate as he glided across Bay Street toward Factors Walk, a tree-shaded sidewalk beside a long line of ancient warehouses once used to store cotton for shipment to Europe in the 1800s, when cotton was king in the south.

The warehouses, now mostly housing restaurants, bars and boutique shops, stretched for a half mile along a high bank on the south side of the Savannah River.

John stepped cautiously down a steep cobblestone street between the warehouses to reach the riverside railing and gaze across the water toward Hutchinson Island.

Torrential rains which fell the previous week in the foothills a hundred or so miles upstream had swollen the river, filling it with flotsam and jetsam like large tree limbs, truck tires, boxes, bottles and other unidentifiable waste riding the swift water which lapped hungrily at the bulkhead beneath the railing.

Mesmerized by the swirling current, John became dizzy as he leaned over the round iron railing to look down on the passing debris racing rapidly to God only knew where.

He squatted behind the lowest iron pipe on the railing to clear his head by scanning the opposite bank, focusing on wind-rippled sawgrass waving rhythmically, water speckling the foliage, causing it to sparkle in the sunshine.

The scene was slowly replaced with thoughts about his new job and speculation about what it might mean for him and Helen.

It would certainly provide him with a legitimate reason to escape from the house early each day, and his earnings would enable him to help Helen. Maybe they could even move out and find an apartment of their own.

Such speculation sucked the afternoon away while John waited for the time Helen would return home after work before heading there himself. He lingered in a dream-like state, savoring progressively more pleasing thoughts until the clock outside the nearby harbor pilot's offices caught his eye.

It was 5 o'clock. Helen would already be home!

John scrambled to his feet and scurried up the hill toward the house, anxious to share his good news, whistling with joy as he walked.

She would be doubly surprised -- by the news of his job and by his early arrival -- since Ben would have told her not to expect him before 6 o'clock.

He hurried faster as he approached the house, undeterred by the sudden acrid, rotten egg smell from the paper mill. Rushing inside, he headed directly for the bedroom, opening the door quietly, hoping to surprise Helen.

He saw her as soon as he entered the room.

She was lying on the bed, the back of her head pressing down into an oversized pillow, her eyes closed and her honey blonde hair framing her face like a soft halo.

But that was the only thing about her that seemed soft at that moment.

Helen's face contorted as her nude body arched upward forming a rigid bridge while her arms stretched above her head, her fingers digging deep into the pillow as moaning sounds emerged from her mouth.

The source of her urgency was Mrs. Creech, who was kneeling with her face buried between Helen's thighs. The loose wrinkles of her aging, chalk white skin appeared grotesque atop Helen's tight smoothness. Her loose, crepe-like flesh quivered as her gray head bobbed rapidly up and down.

Consumed by their own sucking and moaning sounds, neither heard John enter. He stood transfixed, staring in horrified fascination for an excruciatingly long moment before gasping a single word, "Jesus!" before reeling in disgust to stumble out of the room.

Both women froze, paralyzed by the sound of his voice. They remained so for seconds before the full impact penetrated their consciousness.

"Damn you! Damn you!" Helen wailed, turning on Mrs. Creech, slapping her face, head and shoulders again and again while the older woman crouched, defenseless, staring blankly into the face of her young lover.

Tears streamed from both women's eyes.

Finally, still sobbing, Helen collapsed into a pitiful heap where she shuddered uncontrollably as Mrs. Creech staggered out of the room.

Once her sobbing subsided, Helen's shame was supplanted by ominous speculation about the devastating psychological impact the scene must have had on her son.

She wondered where he went. She had no way of knowing that at this moment her son was leaning far out over the riverside rail where he had recently experienced so much joy, joy that seemed a lifetime away now as he stared dizzily down into the rushing water, vomiting in agonizing spasms.

"How could she do that?" he wondered, between aching convulsions that continued long after there was nothing left to regurgitate.

Then, his mind still muddled, he thought he saw Helen's face in the water and leaned out yet further, losing his footing before realizing what he was seeing was the reflection of his own face.

John caught himself on the lowest rail just before plunging into the turbulent river, his brain clearing as he clung to the rail, frightened lucid by his narrow escape as he painstakingly pulled himself back onto the bulkhead.

Resting there, snail-paced reason etched a pattern of understanding across his windowpane mind while he tried to make sense of what he had seen.

Fragments of a picture started filtering through like interconnecting pieces of a puzzle.

Helen was young and beautiful. She had known sex, at least with his father. John, himself was living proof of that. A vital young woman like her would need some sort of sexual release. She couldn't turn those feelings on and off like a faucet. She had to have someone and, having only been with a man who abused her, she was probably afraid to trust another to fill those needs. What other outlet did she have? Mrs. Creech would have been quick to answer that question!

At the same time, John realized it was not just the grotesque scene with Mrs. Creech that tormented him. He felt rejected, felt Helen had forsaken him for someone else and knew he would have felt just as mortified had he found her with a man, worse maybe.

It could have been Ben! The thought made him shudder.

He thought about the misery she must have suffered when he fled the room and realized her pain might even be worse than his own.

He needed to find her, to comfort her, to tell her it was alright. He had to tell her he understood, show her he still loved her. He had to help her right now!

He found himself walking, then running toward the rooming house. It had been two hours since he'd left, and Helen must be frantic. He ran faster, not even slowing his pace as he lurched past Mrs. Creech who was crouching on the front steps weeping, her face in her hands.

John rushed toward the half-open bedroom door, but the strident voices emerging from within stopped him abruptly, just outside.

"Get away from me Ben!" Helen demanded. "Get away now! I don't want you here. Get out."

"Stop pretendin' now," Ben snarled. "I know what ya want. I've knowed for a long time. I seen ya lookin' at me."

"No, Ben. You misunderstood. Believe me. I just wanted to be friends."

Numbed by the words, John couldn't move.

"Aw, get off it Helen. We're all alone. Nobody'll know. Old lady Creech's gone, and so's Johnny. Relax, baby. I know what ya want. You wanta man, needa man, 'n I'm man enough for you. I know ya like my muscles. I got muscles just for you."

John could visualize drool seeping from the corner of Ben's thick lips as he slobbered lecherously over his mother.

"I mean it, Ben," Helen screamed. "Stay away from me!"

"Listen here, Miss Highfalutin. I seen ya goin' to old lady Creech's room. I know what you was doin' in there. You're wastin' yourself baby. You needa man. Ya been shoving that tight little body of yours in my face long enough 'n I'm gonna git it now. I'll do it good. You'll forget all about that old bitch."

"No, Ben no!" Helen pleaded. "Stay away!"

Her plea was followed by muffled sounds of grunting from Ben and the rasping squeak of bed springs protesting the sudden weight of two people along with the sound of ripping of material.

Those sounds marshaled John into motion as if he was poked by an electric cattle prod.

Bursting into the room, he hesitated only a moment when he saw Helen's writhing figure face down, her protesting sounds silenced as Ben forced her face into a pillow.

One of his huge hands held her wrists while the other was clumsily trying to loosen his belt as

Helen squirmed beneath him.

Like a witness, rather than a participant, John observed himself with the heavy brass bedside lamp in his hand, raining blows on Ben's head and shoulders.

He felt detached, oblivious to the blood spurting from the burly man's wounds. Then the lamp was dangling from his hand as he stood silently over the hairy figure lying unconscious on the floor.

Helen, huddled near the foot of the bed, sobbed uncontrollably as John lifted her unresisting body and carried her to the car.

Neither spoke as he spun the rear wheels, launching the old Chevrolet out of the driveway and careened toward the hairpin curve.

About the Author

Born in Atlanta, GA, J. R. Roseberry has resided in the Far East and the eastern U.S. from Florida to New York, with stops in Georgia, South Carolina, Virginia, Tennessee, and Maryland in between.

After living in Atlanta, Knoxville, TN., Anderson and Columbia, SC, as a child, he attended high schools in Pensacola, FL, Rochester, NY, Norfolk, VA, and Leonardtown and St. Mary's City, MD.

Receiving his driver's license at 13, he purchased his first car at 16, the same age at which he became the youngest Red Cross Certified Water Safety Instructor in Maryland and taught swimming classes for dozens of children while also conducting Senior Life Saving courses for college students.

During his senior year in high school he was employed as the Beach Concession Manager, part-time bartender and night cashier at the U.S. Naval Air Station Officer's Club in Patuxent River, MD.

While earning a journalism degree at the University of South Carolina, he won a position as the youngest summer intern at the Atlanta Journal newspaper, then was hired as a full-time staff reporter for The State, South Carolina's largest newspaper, where he was employed throughout his junior and senior years.

Immediately after graduating in 1957, he moved to Tokyo, Japan, where he pursued graduate studies at Sophia University while employed as a reporter and photo editor for Pacific Stars & Stripes, before moving to Okinawa, as an editor for the Okinawa Morning Star and Ryukyu's representative for the Associated Press. While employed at the Star, he designed and served as editor of the paper's monthly entertainment magazine.

Returning to the U.S. in 1961, J.R. became city hall reporter and later Sunday Magazine editor for the Savannah Morning News in Savannah, GA.

He was then hired by the Norfolk Virginian-Pilot, remaining in Norfolk, VA, for five years as reporter and ultimately night city editor before joining the staff of the Washington Post in the nation's capital.

While at the Post, he served as late-night city editor directing coverage of the riots following the assassination of Martin Luther King Jr., before working with Bob Woodward and Carl Bernstein during their Watergate coverage.

J.R. joined a group of key editors in creating the Style section, which featured entertainment, society, and feature stories by nationally-known writers. That section was the first on any major newspaper to replace traditional women's pages, and it proved so successful that it was emulated by every large newspaper in the country.

He then moved to the news desk as Metropolitan News Editor and joined a team of editors working with IBM in one of the initial efforts to incorporate computers in newspaper operations.

After being given the newspaper's newly created title of Production Editor, he re-designed the newspaper, from its former narrow nine columns per page to six columns.

Later, he was named Pre-press Production Manager in which capacity he played a key role in converting the newspaper's production from the historic hot-metal process to cold-type and offset printing.

When the company purchased the Washington Star, which had previously been the country's preeminent afternoon newspaper, J. R. was placed in charge of the Star's facilities where he managed its medical office, restaurant, railroad siding for delivery of newsprint, mailroom, security staff and pressroom.

Under his leadership the plant became the principal printing facility for the Washington Post and won an award for having the best reproduction quality of any newspaper in the entire country utilizing the Napp printing process.

J.R. retired in 1992 after more than 20 years with the Post, then moved to Tybee Island where he returned to his journalistic roots writing a weekly column called "J.R.'s Island View" for the Savannah Morning

News.

The columns were primarily interviews with colorful characters on Tybee Island and the surrounding islands and were later incorporated in a series of three books designed to introduce readers to the people who helped make Tybee the paradise it is today.

He also purchased, published and edited The Tybee News, a tabloid newspaper through which he was able to shine a light on government activities and events which had received little coverage by any other news media.

After selling the paper in the early 2000s, J.R. decided to try his hand at writing fiction and music. Several of his songs have been performed and recorded by area musicians, while his first short story won first place in a competition for writers throughout the Southeast and was published in a Savannah Anthology.

This is his first venture into book-length fiction.

Acknowledgements

I'm deeply indebted to a number of people who contributed to bringing this book to fruition. Among these are:

Savannah Raines, the talented and patient graphic designer and illustrator who created the book's cover as well as the illustrations for each of the stories.

Ben Goggins, Tybee Island author, who served as its principal editor in addition to providing helpful advice and encouragement.

Lauren Clackum, known hereabouts as the Princess of Pages, who did outstanding work on the formatting, layout and technical tasks necessary for publication.

In addition, I want to thank my friends, former wives and chickens who, albeit unwittingly, provided the inspiration which prompted me to write these stories.